Mr. Hornsby
and the
Time-Traveling
Classroom

— BOOK 1 —

SECRETS OF THE PIERCE JOURNAL

ANDREW BREZAK
AND
DANIEL BREZAK

Fulton Books, Inc.
Meadville, PA

Published by Fulton Books 2021

ISBN 978-1-63710-460-6 (paperback)
ISBN 978-1-63710-461-3 (digital)

Printed in the United States of America

1

Becoming a beloved seventh-grade history teacher at Upper Kakapo Middle School had always been Mr. Ethan Hornsby's dream.

Not only was the school filled with the kindest teachers, but the students also were awesome, and even better, the giant library was filled with historical reference books on every shelf, containing all the history one could enjoy. This was how he had felt when he was an ultra-shy, fluffy-haired, slightly out of shape student walking these same halls years ago. And it was the same way he felt now as a straight out of college, wanna-get-hired, freshly bearded, glasses, shiny tie-wearing, and newly certified social studies teacher.

But now came the giant hurdle. He had to prove himself first as a substitute teacher.

It seemed everyone just looooved Mr. Slattery so much more—that striking celebrity smile, his perfectly combed, glistening blond hair, the ultracool personality that had students running to guidance to request him. Where did he get all those funny jokes?

Mr. Hornsby could only dream that one day, he would be able to light up a room just like Mr. Slattery. Instead, he seemed to always trip upon entrance over a racing heart, the beaded curtain of sweat on his forehead, and his fumbling words.

"Maybe they'll let you stay here as a student." Slattery laughed at him as they passed each other in the art hallway. "You're certainly never going to be allowed to stay as a teacher."

Mr. Slattery was like this when they were in school together as kids. He got away with it then, and it seemed he would get away with it forever.

And then there was Mrs. Peacock, the principal, with her buoyant manicured curls, which she dyed gold as if to melt them for fortune, and that iced-laser stare. You couldn't scoot past her without feeling it on the back of your head. And the intimidating tones—some students swore she must have been Cruella de Vil in her past life, though Hornsby thought she sounded more like the voice of Ursula from the animated version of *The Little Mermaid*.

"How are you ever going to get kids to do well on our state exams, Hornsby? More boring stories about ex-presidents while our students stare out windows?"

"Yes, ma'am. I mean, no, ma'am."

"Maybe you should find another purpose for all that historical information you have locked up in your brain, because this is middle school. If the students can't connect with you on a more childish level, you will remain useless to me."

Just then, Mr. Slattery walked on by. He always seemed to have that knack for perfect timing. "Why, hello, Mr. Slattery."

"Hello, Mrs. Peacock. Is there any way I can help you again today?"

Brown noser.

"Why, thank you, Mr. Slattery. You're always so helpful. It won't be long before I can find"—Mrs. Peacock seemed to revel at, staring Mr. Hornsby right in the eyes—"a more permanent position here at Upper Kakapo for you."

"Yes, of course, Mrs. Peacock."

"If I need any help, I know who to reach out to. Thank you, Mr. Slattery."

As Slattery walked away, he gave Hornsby a wink. Of course, he did.

"You see that, Mr. Hornsby. Show me that you've got what he's got. Until then"—she handed over a key to room A 109—"you will remain just a fill-in for my *real* teachers."

Off Mr. Hornsby went to room A 109. This was Mrs. Keptoe's room, an eighth-grade US history teacher.

Mrs. Keptoe's room had it all—the brand-new touch SMART board for learning on the wall, that comfortable cushy leather chair, the beanbags, the mats, and even modern desks that rose if students wanted to stand. There was even a set of laptops spread out across a rectangular table in the back. And the absolute coolest posters of important historical events on the walls were also there—General Lee surrendering to General Grant at Appomattox to end the Civil War, firefighters pushing up a torn American flag after September 11, and soldiers during World War II hoisting an American flag at Iwo Jima.

And yet, as Hornsby turned the key, he saw something quite different.

He entered instead to find an unsanded wooden plank floor, one small teacher's desk made of steel, and a wooden chair that looked like it was built by a custodian. The chalkboard was only a tiny square that looked like it was made out of slate by fourth-graders for a project, no less, and the wooden walls were barren. Everything smelled of sawdust. Hornsby counted only four rows of wooden tables in the middle of the room with chairs.

But what was even more alarming than the appearance of the room was that there were already students sitting at the tables. And yet students were never allowed into the building before eight o'clock in the morning.

Mr. Hornsby, of course, rushed next door to Mrs. Kimmelman's room to ask her about it. She followed him in. "What?"

"Don't you see?"

"See what?"

"What happened to Mrs. Keptoe's room?"

"Looks normal to me?"

"But where's her SMART board?"

Mrs. Kimmelman pointed. "Right there."

"Where?"

"There."

"And where are the laptops?"

Mrs. Kimmelman pointed at them. "You okay, Mr. Hornsby?"

"Yeah, why?" Mr. Hornsby continued to look around, still unable to find any of the technology. He rubbed his beard. "And who are these students?"

Mrs. Kimmelman was even more puzzled. "Which students?"

"Them. The kids at the tables."

"Haha, who put you up to this? Mr. Slattery?"

"No one put me up to it."

Mrs. Kimmelman began to walk out of the classroom. She turned. "That Slattery. Well, you let him know I'm not falling for any more of his practical jokes. Nice try, guys." Kimmelman giggled. "Have a great day, Mr. Hornsby."

This was befuddling. Hornsby looked again at the young teen boys, each sitting quietly and proper, wearing long pants with maroon sweaters and the large letters BRA stitched on the fronts. But what was even crazier was that they weren't playing on their cell phones.

Mr. Hornsby looked up and down the Upper Kakapo hallways as the morning bell sounded. Here came all the rest. Every one of them looked normal, way more up to date with their styles than the boys in his room. Mr. Hornsby looked again at the tables of students. There weren't any backpacks either. He remained by the door, unable to understand any of this. Outside of his classroom door, everything seemed completely normal. Yet inside of the classroom walls, it was like he was staring at an old picture belonging inside an antique frame.

He checked one more time across the hallway, but both of those rooms still had their SMART boards on the walls and laptops at their tables. Everything was bright and cheery. He put his hands through his brown hair, adjusted his too loose for his collar tie (because he could never get the top button closed), reached into his pocket for another bite of his candy bar, and headed inside. Now the second bell rang, which meant class should be underway.

"Shall I close the door?" one of the boys asked.

"Yeah, sure, close the door."

Just then, a stocky silver-haired gentleman, wearing a gray wool suit with a derby-styled hat came rushing in through the outside door that connected to the field. "Mr. Hornsby, you finally made it. I was told you might be late."

"You were?"

"Begget is the name. And I am the headmaster here at Black River Academy in Vermont."

"Where?"

"I was informed that my secretary had provided you with everything you will need for the day on your desk. If there is anything else, please send one of the pupils down to my office. And thank you, Mr. Hornsby." Mr. Begget lifted his cap. "And good day, sir."

"Okay... Mr. Begget."

Mr. Begget exited through the back door.

Mr. Hornsby was even more baffled now. He walked back over to the main door and stepped back out into the hallway. Once again, everything on that side of the classroom seemed totally normal. He walked over to the steel desk and dropped himself into the uncomfortable wooden chair. He finished his candy bar. "Maybe Mr. Slattery really is this good at playing practical jokes," he mused.

Wait a minute, Hornsby thought to himself. *Surely outside will look normal. There must be cars in the lot and ballfields and everything else to adore about Upper Kakapo.* But his body froze when he crossed to the windows and looked out. Nothing but farmland and two sets of horses and buggies tied up to stakes.

"Okay, Hornsby," he said to himself. "This is just a dream. It's not real. Keep your head. At any moment, you'll wake up. Maybe try to count sheep or something."

But nothing changed, and there was no waking up.

Mr. Begget mentioned that everything he would need would be on the desk. He made his way back over and found a roster of students. There was also a calendar. Today was September 14, 1884.

"Mr. Hornsby, may we read now?" one of the boys respectfully asked.

"What?"

"May we read now, Mr. Hornsby."

Hornsby looked around. "Read what?"

"We would like to grab our Bibles and slate tablets from the closet."

Hornsby fell back into his chair. "Oh yeah, sure, Bibles and slate tablets."

Hornsby wanted to splash water on his face to wake himself out of this nightmare, but since he had no access to a fountain, he instead gave himself the loudest slap right across his own face. The boys couldn't help themselves and burst out in laughter. Hornsby offered a smile. "Pretty funny to you guys, huh?" He picked up the roster of names. "What's a guy gotta do for some light in this place?" He walked over by the door, but there was no light switch. He headed over to the windows and used the sunshine to call out each of their names.

But he stopped at the third name on the roster, Calvin Coolidge.

His eyes shifted over to the date of birth then back to the name then back to the date of birth. He quickly added the years up in his head, trying to assess how old this Calvin Coolidge would be by the year 1923 when a person by the same name would be sworn in as the thirtieth president of the United States. "It can't be. No way. It can't be," he said to himself. But the dates did match up.

He called out the name. "Calvin Coolidge."

But none of the boys answered.

He called out the name again. "Calvin Coolidge?"

"He's probably outside under that tree again," one of the boys said.

Hornsby looked closely out of the window. His eyes located the humungous oak tree on the right with its thick, monstrous branches.

There he was.

2

Hornsby watched as young Calvin was pulling grass and tossing it into the wind. "Does your teacher usually go out there to bring him in?"

"Mr. Chester is never pleased. He used to bring him inside. Now he's been threatening to have him expelled," said one of the boys. "Mr. Coolidge, his father, was here the other day."

Hornsby began to walk out the door but immediately stopped short. By stepping outside, what might happen? Would he be stuck outside in the year 1884 forever? What about his health? Would the air be different on his lungs? What if he tripped and fell in this old world? Could he get proper medical care? What if the townsfolk saw how he was dressed and took him for a dangerous stranger?

But then he thought about all those years upon years when he sat in a chair as a kid reading through all those historical books in the Upper Kakapo Middle School library and how many books and papers he went on to write in college about important men and women. And right there in front of him sat a boy who was going to be president during the famous Roaring Twenties. The man the world would come to know as "Silent Cal."

He began to take a step toward the outside. But then one of the boys asked, "Mr. Hornsby?"

"Yes?"

"May we go get our Bibles and slate tablets now?"

"Yeah, sure. Why not? Go get 'em."

The boys all stood up at the same time and began to make their way to the closet. "Now wait a second, boys. Hasn't Mr. Chester assigned jobs for this kind of stuff?"

The boys appeared puzzled. "No."

"Okay, you two. What are your names?"

"William Tinder, sir."

"Mathew Augustine, sir."

"Okay, from now on, you two will be in charge of collecting Bibles and tablets from the closet—only you two. And you will distribute to the others. The rest of you have a seat."

"Have a seat, sir?" another boy asked.

"Yes, have a seat."

"What do I do with it, sir? Take it home?"

Hornsby laughed. "No…no…it's just an expression. It means take your seat. No. What I mean is…please sit down." The boys sat. "Augustine, you will also be in charge this week of selecting the passage for everyone to read."

"What's that by your side?" William Tinder asked.

"You mean this?" Hornsby held up his iPhone.

"Yes."

At first, Hornsby went to tuck it right back into his pocket. *These boys will only live to see the traditional phone, not the cell phone, certainly not any smartphones.* At this point, though, he thought a little harmless fun could be his recipe for laughter. He began to speak like a ringmaster as if he was in front of a large circus crowd, "Gentlemen, this is an ultra-modern, most amazingly efficient, supernatural, highly effective"—Hornsby raised up his finger—"transportation machine!"

"It is?" one of the boys asked.

"It is. All I have to do is press this button right here, and a horse and carriage will come to pick me up to take me wherever I want to go."

"What's it called?"

"You mean this app, right here? It's called Uber."

"I have to tell Pa about this," a boy said.

"You should tell Mr. Chester too. Oh, and while you're telling him about Uber, you can tell Mr. Chester that this button right here allows me to send a message to anyone, anywhere."

"Using Morse code?" Tinder asked.

"Yes, sir. I can send a Morse coded message to anyone. But the other person also needs one of these."

"Where do you get one?"

But Hornsby was once again lost in his thoughts, as he continued to stare at the phone, unable to turn it on in this old world. Yet when he walked out into the hallway, it powered up. He was truly confused by his purpose for being in an 1884 classroom. "I'm sorry, boys, I have absolutely no idea what I'm supposed to be doing right now or why I have been chosen to be your teacher today." He sat down, his tone deflated. "Just read. Please. Everyone just read your Bibles."

The boys began to read quietly. *This is one well-behaved group*, Hornsby thought, as each student stayed on task. That they were learning from Bibles did at least make sense for the era, since most schools during this time period had such few other books to provide.

Hornsby looked at the closet and wondered if there were any clues inside it that could make this all stop. He walked over. Besides the extra Bibles and tablets, there were small erasers that looked like they were made with some type of animal fur. He carried one over to his blackboard, took a piece of chalk, and drew a line. He then tested to see how effective this eraser was at erasing. *Not bad*, he thought, *for animal fur*.

Hornsby continued to ask himself what he was supposed to be doing. Should he go find Mr. Begget and look for clues in his office? Or maybe he should grab hold of one of the horses out there and ride it into town to see what else was around. Of course, he had no idea how to ride one, so that was immediately off the table. He walked over by the window. The only part of this journey that had some recognition was the boy that was sitting against the tree.

And so Mr. Hornsby—the chubby, bearded, glasses-wearing, and shiny tie-wearing rookie substitutive teacher who dreamed about teaching history to middle school students—walked back over to the outside door and took the leap, stepping outside into another unknown world.

But the wind against his face felt exactly the same.

So did the grass under his feet.

And the sounds? Well, it was certainly quieter than what he normally heard outside of Upper Kakapo Middle School. He turned to look at the building. No longer was there a modern school made of bricks, with wonderfully fastened large windows and modern solar panels on the rooftop. Gone were all the blacktop and the cozy sign that welcomed students and parents every morning. What sat instead in this spot was the framework of what was probably at one time a church. There was a large cross sitting atop. Many feet away appeared to be a beaten-down storage barn. Then there was that dusty road. It seemed to just go on for miles across wide-open fields.

Hornsby wondered how far each of these kids walked to get here every morning.

The wind picked up. Of course, it would, as everything was so much more open.

Hornsby approached the boy, who looked so sad. Suddenly, every time-traveling movie he watched and every book he read began to play in his mind. "Do not alter history," he whispered silently. Or was that his purpose for being here?

Hornsby sat down next to Cal. "My name's Mr. Hornsby. I'm your teacher for today."

"Are you going to take the wooden stick to me like Mr. Chester?"

Wooden stick? Oh my god!

Hornsby did recall seeing one against the wall in the corner of the classroom. He knew from his studies students back then faced corporal punishment from teachers, as they would be hit and paddled on their backsides if they misbehaved. "No way, Calvin. Not me. I would never do that to you." Calvin looked up with relief. "Because you're not misbehaving."

"I'm not?"

"No. You've done nothing wrong. It's important that we all take time for ourselves each day. That's all you're doing. Now I want you to look up into the sky for me and try to find a cloud."

"Okay."

"One day we'll be up there flying. Men and women."

"Like birds?"

"Like birds. I know this because, right about now, there are two brothers, Wilbur and Orville Wright, who are just a bit older than you are. But they go to bed every night dreaming about making a machine that can fly. And I know these two brothers won't give up until they show the world they've done it." Hornsby pointed again. "And do you see that long dirt road?"

"Yes."

"The time will come when we don't need to use horses anymore to travel that road because of young men like Henry Ford." Hornsby quickly calculated how old Ford would currently be. "He's right now twenty-one years old. Not much older than any of you boys. But he also goes to bed every night with dreams that one day he can change the world. And he will. Actually, right now, in a faraway land known as the country of Germany, a man by the name of Karl Benz is working on this horseless carriage and is really close to making it work. By next year, actually, he'll be able to drive it around. No horses!"

"My pa never said anything about this."

"I know of your pa. He's a very successful merchant, an important man in town. That's why you get to be dressed up so nicely and get to go to school like this, while other boys are stuck home working on their farms. You're expected to go one day to college. But your pa is also like my pa. They know a lot. But they don't know everything."

"He told me if I don't start going inside to the classroom, he's going to take me out of school to work the farm instead."

"If Karl Benz can push himself to create a horseless carriage, then you can push yourself to walk inside there."

"No horses? Really?"

"No horses needed. In the next couple of years, we'll also be getting inventions like the steam iron to press away wrinkles from clothes and even the thermostat, so we'll know how cold or warm it is."

"I just put my face out the window each day."

"That works also." Hornsby laughed. "But, Calvin, this is all going to take place because dreams don't just happen at night. They also happen during the day."

"I don't really like the daytime anymore."

"Why?" But Calvin wouldn't say.

"What do you dream of, Calvin?"

Calvin shrugged his shoulders. "To not be afraid to go in there, I guess."

Hornsby asked a question, though he knew from history what the answer already was. "Are you really shy, Calvin?"

"What's that mean?"

"It means you can get nervous when around others."

"I do get nerves."

"And this makes you unhappy?"

"Yes."

"And your pa has told you that it's wrong to feel this way?"

"Yes. And my teachers whip me for it."

"But it's not wrong to feel this way. It's very right actually to be shy."

"I'm sorry, Mr. Hornsby, but that isn't the case. It's a terrible way to be. My pa assures me of it."

"Okay, I want you to do something for me. Inside the others are reading their Bibles. They will see you come through the door but won't pay much attention once you sit down. We will pretend as if you are going to your seat but instead head into the closet."

"You want me to go into the closet?"

"I do. There's a space for you next to the Bibles. Stay in there and wait for me to tell the others to stop reading. At that point, I'll call upon a couple of the students to collect the Bibles and put them back. But I will open the closet for them. When I open it up, give me a big scare!"

Calvin smiled. "Why?"

"To make the others laugh, that's why. I can use a good laugh as well. I want a heart attack-type scare."

"What's a heart attack?"

"Don't worry, just give a good scare. Okay?"

Calvin smiled wide.

"And one other thing. While in that closet, I want you to think about something you know more about than any other boy in that room."

"That's easy. I know more about my pa's store than anyone."

"Good. After our little practical joke, I'm going to put you up there in front of the others to make a speech about it."

"Oh no, Mr. Hornsby. I'm never doing that."

"Did I ever tell you that it was wrong to be shy?"

"No."

"Did I say you needed to change who you are or how you feel?"

"No."

"Because you're not wrong and I never want you to change. I want you to be exactly who you are."

"But if I'm going to be giving a speech in front of others, then I need time to really think about it. It has to be done right. I want to practice it first so I won't have nerves."

"Ahhh, and there it is, Calvin. You just figured out how to use who you are as an advantage. In the future, I'd make a bet that there'll be one of the greatest orators to ever live who becomes president of the United States. All because he was shy and afraid."

"What's an orator?"

"He's someone who's really good at giving speeches. He works hard on writing them. He prepares extra with practice. He even might stand in front of mirrors to practice. All because he's scared to death about what would happen if he didn't." Hornsby paused. "Okay, I won't make you go up there today. I'll give you more time to prepare to meet that higher standard you've set. But let's get in there to play that practical joke."

Calvin was smiling wide once again. "Okay."

Hornsby watched as Calvin entered the building. He followed him inside, then suddenly it was all gone.

Vanished were the boys with their maroon school sweaters and Bibles. Gone was the hodgepodge chalkboard, the old desk and chair, the wooden-plank floor.

Back instead was the SMART board and computers.

There was Mrs. Keptoe's class staring at him. Each kid was sitting in his or her seat.

Also, there was Mrs. Peacock standing in the middle of the room, tapping her hand against her thigh.

She did not look happy.

3

"Mr. Hornsby, may I please speak with you out in the hallway?"

Freaking out, Hornsby followed his principal out to the hallway. On his way to the door, he couldn't help but see that most of the kids had their cellphones out, while on the teacher's desk, there were stacks of dittos that hadn't been distributed. He wondered if there could be worse crimes committed by a substitute teacher, but Mrs. Peacock quickly provided his answer. "Mr. Hornsby, there is no greater crime committed by one of my teachers than leaving students unattended."

Hornsby tried to think of how to explain this without blundering his words. "I can explain...no, I can't... I mean, I can...but you would never—"

"What in the world were you thinking, leaving them alone while you were outside?"

"Actually... I gave it quite some thought before going outside. What I mean is, I wasn't thinking. No, actually I was thinking—"

Peacock interrupted, "Mrs. Keptoe provided clear and concise plans, but we are already two periods into the day, and it looks like you haven't even handed out one assignment?"

"See that's the thing... I didn't see any plans." *Ouch*, Hornsby thought. He didn't think this could get any worse, but it actually was. "I mean, what I'm trying to say is, I didn't see the desk. I mean..."

Mrs. Peacock stepped in closer. Hornsby could feel and smell her hot cinnamon gum-chewing breath. "The only reason you were even hired to begin with is that Mr. Waters saw you were once a student here. If it was up to me, I never would have even conducted the interview."

"I understand, ma'am."

Peacock poked her finger into Hornsby's chest. "This is your last chance."

"Yes, ma'am."

The next period was a prep period, and Hornsby bolted straight for the library. There, sitting behind the desk, was Rosie Mizrack, who was not only the school's librarian but also was the kid from down the block of Hornsby's childhood, always on her dirt bike, always with dirt on her knees, and always with dirt around the brim of her baseball cap. But now Hornsby saw her in a completely different light, realizing how pretty she always was.

Hornsby gazed around the library. All the computers were occupied by students. "Can I please use yours, Rosie?"

Rosie could sense the desperation. "Everything okay, Ethan?"

"I just have to look something up."

Hornsby wanted to see if he could find pictures of Calvin Coolidge as a boy so he would know for sure if that really was him sitting beside that oak tree. But not only could he not find any pictures of Calvin, the kid, but also nothing had even come up about Calvin, the thirtieth president of the United States. "But how could that be?" Hornsby whispered under his breath.

"You sure everything is okay?"

"Rosie, please point me in the direction of any book on the shelves about President Calvin Coolidge."

Rosie sat down at the reference computer and began a search. "How do you spell his last name?"

Hornsby pointed at the screen. "You have it right."

"Can't be. There's nothing coming up."

"Try John Coolidge. He only went by his middle name Calvin."

"Still nothing."

"But how can that be?"

"You sure about this guy? I've never heard of him."

"Are you really questioning *my* knowledge of our thirtieth president?"

"Well, sorry there, *Mr. History Expert.* What I mean is, maybe since he's not as well-known as the big ones like Washington, Lincoln, or Roosevelt, our library isn't carrying anything on him. "

"It has in the past. I've read them all here. Maybe try looking up general reference books about the presidents. He was in the White House from 1923–1929. It was during one of the most prosperous economic booms in our nation's history."

"Nope. Nothing. Says here it was Mr. John W. Davis who was president."

"What?"

"The book is right over there on that shelf."

Hornsby rushed over. He quickly started to turn the pages. "No, no...how can that have happened?"

"How could what have happened?" asked Rosie.

Hornsby had his head in his hands. "What did I do?"

"Please, Ethan. You have to tell me what's going on."

"I wish I could. I mean, you're the only person in this entire building who's actually believed in me in my life. So I want to. But I don't really understand it myself."

"Does it have something to do with Mrs. Peacock?"

"In a way, yes."

"Because I was on her hit list at one point in my first year. I know how it feels."

"I don't think anyone can know how I'm feeling right now."

"I figured out how to weave my way out of trouble with her. So maybe if you tell me what happened, I can help."

"But you'll think I'm nuts. Like beyond crazy!"

"Maybe I already do." Rosie laughed.

Hornsby laughed as well. "Well, Calvin Coolidge was so important to many kids through the years because he was one of the few introverts to become president. They called him 'Silent Cal.'"

"I take it from the nickname, he didn't talk much. Is that what you mean by introverted?"

"Yes. Some presidents were shyer and quieter than others— Thomas Jefferson for one. But Calvin preferred to really keep to himself. That's why he's so important to the history books. He showed people it's okay to be a bit of a loner and still be just as successful as anyone else."

"How did he do it?"

"He's known for being one of the biggest practical jokers ever in the White House. If you got to know him, he had a really good sense of humor. And he was tremendous at giving speeches. He was always well prepared. He also had the media give him questions ahead of time so he wouldn't be nervous. But I screwed it all up."

"How could you screw it up? Coolidge must be dead for many years already."

"I traveled through time."

And there was that face that Hornsby was expecting from Rosie, the one where she looked at him like he was delirious. "I told you you'd think I was crazy."

"How could you have traveled through time?"

"I can't really explain why or how for any of it. But I met him. He was so young. And I tried to help him. But like everything else, I even managed to screw up something that was etched in the history books."

"You think you altered history?"

"John W. Davis was the man who Coolidge defeated in the election of 1924. But even before that, Coolidge was Warren Harding's vice president until Harding's death, and then Coolidge took over as president. But there is not even a record of that." Hornsby looked Rosie in the eyes. "I knew you wouldn't believe me."

"Would you?"

"No. So I can't blame you. If someone told me this story, I wouldn't believe them either. But it happened. I swear. But I didn't mean to hurt Calvin. I got sent back right before I could complete my lesson with him. Something must have gone wrong."

"How old was he in this time-traveling world?"

"It was 1884. He was twelve." Hornsby placed his head back in his hands. "He was one of my favorite presidents because I just loved his quotes. He was famous for saying, 'It takes a great man to be a good listener.' People don't want to listen anymore. They just want to talk and be heard."

"That's a nice quote. He was twelve, huh? What was he like?"

"So you do believe me. I can hear it in your voice."

"I want to…believe you… I really do."

"Wait, what did you just ask me?"

"You mean he was twelve, huh?"

"Yes. He was twelve."

"Okay?"

"That's it! He was twelve!"

Rosie looked even more confused now.

"I *have* to figure out how to get back to him. I can fix this! He was twelve! He was twelve!"

"So what's the big deal about being twelve?"

"It's not a big deal for most. But if my historical knowledge is accurate, being twelve was a huge deal for him. And that's what I messed up. His quote… I talked…and talked…but what I didn't do was really listen to him. He was trying to tell me something. I really gotta get back there." Hornsby paused. "Find out which class I'm covering tomorrow. And meet me in that room, first thing. I promise you'll see. It'll be worth it."

"Okay."

"I gotta go, Rosie! Thank you so much!"

Rosie put her hands up. "But I didn't do anything."

"See you tomorrow. And don't forget! Find me. I'll prove everything I said is real. And I plan on fixing our nation's history!"

4

But who else would stop Hornsby short in his tracks in the hallway except Mr. Slattery?

"Why, hello there, *Thorns*by."

Slattery shifted his body to stay in front each time Hornsby tried to pass. "Please, let me pass."

But Slattery still would not budge. "I want to show you my crystal ball." Slattery pretended as if he had a ball in his hand, and he made motions with his fingers all around it. "Look into it, *Thorns*by. You see? It's our future. Ted Jones is just about to put in his retirement papers, meaning there will be a social studies job opening up. Now look closer at my hands. Our future is clear. It will be *me* getting that job."

"Just please let me walk past."

Mr. Slattery looked Hornsby up and down. "You know what? I actually pity you, *Thorns*by. Someone like you will always need assistance from someone like me. So I'm going to share a little bit of important information with you, the lifesaving kind."

"I'm not asking for your help."

"But you know, us guys on top should always look out for those below."

"Please. I just want to get back to my room."

"Oh, now it's *your* room? Is it?"

"Okay, Slattery. What important information do you feel is vital to share with me, just so I can be forever indebted to you?"

Slattery took a step closer. He then looked around to make sure no one could hear them. "Old Man Waters is not only in the building right now, but also I've been informed that he's popping into classrooms to get a look-see at the new substitutes. You know, to see if any of us show promise. And that means a visit to both you and me."

Hornsby felt the nerves in his belly explode.

Old Man Waters was Benjamin Waters, superintendent of schools, the man who had presided over this district, it seemed since dinosaurs roamed. He was also the final vote in the hiring process of new teachers. One false move, as legend had it, and he would hold it against you forever.

"Now tell me the *real* reason you actually decided to help me for a change," said Hornsby.

"Let's just say I want to beat you at this fair and square like I always have in everything we've ever competed in. And let's just say I remain very confident that even with this advanced notice, you'll never be able to match my standards. Game on, *Thorns*by." Slattery stepped aside to allow him to pass.

Hornsby, though, had to take a moment to catch his breath from the anxiety. This day was officially a horror movie, as now the threat of Old Man Waters walking into his classroom hovered like a dark cloud.

He made it back to his classroom just as the bell was ringing. The next group of students were on their way.

And Hornsby had an idea.

He would remain at the doorway, not only to welcome the next class in but also to instruct them. As much as he wanted to step inside to see if he could make it back to Calvin, he also had to ensure that active learning was taking place in his real class. "Hello, everyone, I am Mr. Hornsby."

"Why are you standing out there?" asked one of the kids.

Hornsby did his best to ignore the question. "Okay, I need a volunteer. Can someone please pass out a set of dittos for me?"

"I will," volunteered a girl from the front row.

"Okay, they're on the desk."

"Which ones should I pass out? There are three different piles."

From the hallway, Hornsby said, "Hold them up so I can see." He squinted with his eyes but couldn't read them.

The same boy asked again, "Why are you standing out there?"

"Which ones?" asked the girl.

"Just bring them to me."

But Hornsby meant only one sheet from each pile, not to try to lift all three at the same time. But, of course, he could do nothing to stop it. It felt like it was happening in slow motion, the girl trying to lift all three piles at the same time, dropping papers all over the floor.

"Hello there, Mr. Hornsby."

Oh no, please. Not right now.

It was the soft, deep voice of Old Man Waters who was now directly behind him. Quickly throwing on a massive smile, Hornsby turned. "Hi, Mr. Waters."

Old Man Waters was continuing to roll out the same suits as yesteryear, even though he no longer filled them out and obviously shrunk an inch or two. He was bald down to the smallest hairline around the ears and had age spots all around his scalp, like scattered stars around a galaxy. One of the spots was covered with a small Band-Aid. Waters had a cancerous spot removed in the morning and still showed up to hold his noon meeting.

"I saw from the scheduling you're filling in today for Mrs. Keptoe."

"Yes, sir. I am."

"May I come inside to watch how you are managing the class?"

"Managing away," Hornsby gestured, snapping his fingers. "Management. Gotta have it!"

A girl from the middle of the classroom asked, "Mr. Hornsby, may I help Claudia pick up the papers?" Claudia was already on her knees, trying to scoop them up.

"Yes, please. And thank you." Hornsby turned. "See, managing like a manager."

"May we please go inside now?"

"In *there*?" Hornsby asked the superintendent.

"*Where else?*"

Hornsby held up his hands. "I mean, why not just talk out here?" He waved to a student walking past.

"Because I'm not here to talk." He pointed. *"And I want us to go in there."*

"Look at them, they're getting their dittos now…all cleaned up…team effort…and there will be learning…lots…*lots* of learning. Can't beat this bird's-eye view, can you?"

"I want to see how you circle the classroom and interact with the students."

"Been circling all day, sir." Hornsby used his fingers to draw in the air. "Circles here, circles there. Lots of circling. Circled my way right out to the hallway, in fact. Even squared around the building a couple of times."

"If I didn't know any better, Mr. Hornsby, I would think you were trying to hide something from me."

"Oh no, sir."

"Well, I'm going inside now. And I would expect to see a teacher in the room once I get there." Old Man Waters entered and headed for an empty desk in the back row. Hornsby anxiously lifted his right foot in the air to try to take a step forward but just held it in place, afraid to place it down on the other side of the door.

But he did.

And nothing changed. Everything was still normal.

A very important light bulb went on inside Hornsby's head as he had learned something critically important about this new time-traveling power. If an adult was already present inside the room, his ability was halted.

For the first time all day, Mr. Hornsby was ready to breathe a sigh of relief.

And yet, all that he could feel, as Mr. Waters stared from the back of the room, was self-doubt—just as Calvin had under that tree.

5

"Come quick!" Hornsby tried to wave Rosie over.

But Rosie was stuck behind the large checkout desk in the library with students all around. New classes were packing the library once again. "You said to find you in the morning."

"But I think I just discovered something. And I really need you to help me retest my theory."

Rosie felt exhausted as she looked around the noisy library then at all the piles of books she still hadn't gotten to and then over at each of the kids still waiting for attention. She could feel the pull from Hornsby though and sensed that whatever wackiness he had in store just might be exactly what the doctor ordered. She leaned over to Ms. Bean, one of the teachers who was assigned to help out, and said, "Be right back."

They reached Hornsby's room. "Okay, you enter the room first, and then I'll follow."

"Why?"

"Just a theory I need to retest."

"Okay." Rosie entered. Then Hornsby followed.

"See?"

"See what?"

"I didn't travel back in time. Because an adult is already in the room."

"Okay, now what?"

"Now I need your help to see what exactly is taking place in this room when I do go back in time. Mrs. Peacock yelled at me that I had left my students unattended. But I just need to be sure that you don't see me while I'm back in 1884."

"Then where do you need me?"

"Stand out here in the hall. I'll enter alone. Let's see what happens. If I do travel back in time, I promise I'll be right back."

"Okay. Go ahead."

Hornsby entered the room by himself and was immediately transformed back into the one-room schoolhouse. But this time, there were no students. Calvin was nowhere to be found. He quickly walked back out. "And?"

"And what?"

"Like what happened?"

"You sat down at the desk and picked up a book."

"I did?"

"Didn't you?"

"No. I was back in 1884."

"Really? But how's that possible?"

"I'm not sure yet. Did you try to talk with me?"

"Was I supposed to?"

"I guess not."

"But it was you, all right."

"But it wasn't."

"I'm so confused right now. How are you in two places at once?"

"I'm even more confused now myself. So when Peacock entered, she didn't see me. But when it was you standing outside, you saw some phantom version of me, let's say, sit down at the desk and pick up a book to read?"

"I guess so."

"Could you tell which book it was?"

"I didn't think to look."

Hornsby tried to process it all. Just then, without warning, he grabbed Rosie's hand and stepped back into the classroom. Suddenly, Rosie was also with him in 1884.

"Oh my god," she said.

"It worked! I knew it! Ha ha! I just knew it would work!" Hornsby danced around the room as Rosie remained in shock. "I just had this feeling that if you held my hand, as I came through, you would go back in time with me."

Rosie knelt down to touch the unfinished wooden plank floor. She made her way over by the door, feeling along the wooden walls, seeing that there was no light switch. Then she felt around the old desk and chair. She looked up at the slate chalkboard. "Oh my god."

"I know. The initial shock of it is a bit overwhelming."

Rosie looked at the empty tables. "Where is everyone?"

"Must have left for the day."

They both sat down to observe the quiet. "This is what 1884 sounds like?"

"Yeah, it's really peaceful. Go look outside the window."

"Wow."

"Welcome to Vermont."

"So we not only traveled back in time but we also switched locations?"

"Yep."

Rosie sat back down. "But why? Why is this happening?"

"I think this has something to do with when I was just a kid. I used to sit in my classes, so unhappy with myself, feeling so insecure around others, like I never belonged."

"I'm so sorry you went through that."

"But the one thing I always had were my history books. I'd read and read all about the important people in our nation's history. And I would dream, wishing that I would be whisked away back in time to their worlds."

"What were you hoping for?"

"That somehow I'd be important like them, that I'd mean something. That maybe their worlds would accept me more."

"Then you're wrong, Ethan. You aren't just traveling to 1884 to help Calvin. You're traveling back in time to help yourself."

"But that was only silly kid stuff. I'm an adult now. I don't need to be here anymore. And I'm trying to get Mrs. Peacock and Old Man Waters to take me seriously enough to give me a full-time teaching job. And now this will only get in my way."

"Then how can you make it stop?"

"That's what I have to find out."

"And what if Calvin is only the beginning?" Rosie asked. "What if there are other time periods to come?"

Suddenly, the loud voices of children approached the building. Hornsby peaked out of the window. It was his class of boys being led back by Mr. Begget. "They're returning. I see Calvin."

"I should get back anyway," said Rosie. "Who knows if there's some phantom of me sitting in a library right now." Rosie paused, seeing worry on Hornsby's face. "What's the matter, Ethan?"

"I'm feeling really nervous again, all of a sudden."

"Why?"

"What if I can't help Calvin? What if I keep doing the wrong thing?"

"I've known you forever, Ethan. You have a heart of gold."

Hornsby peeked out the window, still feeling a lack of confidence. "Before you go"—he reached into the closet and handed her a Bible—"let's see if we can take old mementos back with us. Or else we'll never have proof."

Rosie accepted the Bible. "Now go fix history back to the way it was supposed to be." She stepped back into the hallway, but the Bible would not pass through. It landed on the wooden floor. Hornsby picked it up, placing it back in the closet.

"Mr. Hornsby, there you are," said Mr. Begget. "The pupils said you left for the day. I took them outside for some games."

"I did have a bit of an emergency. Thank you, Mr. Begget, for keeping them busy until I returned."

"Grab your pencils and head home now," Begget said to the boys. "We'll see you tomorrow."

"Tinder, Augustine, and Coolidge, come here."

The three boys approached. Hornsby thanked the first two for helping him earlier and sent them on their way. "You stay here, Calvin. You and I need to talk."

6

"I'm so sorry for leaving you in the closet. What wound up happening?"

"So much time went by, and the door never opened up. I just got out and sat down in my seat."

"I blew it. I should have been there for you to get a good laugh."

"It's okay, Mr. Hornsby."

Hornsby led Calvin back out to the tree. "But the way I really wasn't there for you was the last time we were out here. A very important man once said, 'It takes a great man to be a good listener.' And that was my mistake. I did too much talking and not enough listening."

Hornsby paused. He remembered that Calvin was twelve, which meant that his mother just passed away. This was one of the worst years of his life. Calvin didn't need a cheap laugh from some practical joke. What he needed was someone to be there for him. "But I'm ready to just be your listener now."

Suddenly, Calvin began to break down and cry. It started off slow, but within a few seconds, there was the release of real anguish. His face was covered in tears. "I thought about that speech you wanted me to give."

"No, no...don't you worry one bit about that."

"But I wrote it in my head. While the others were playing, I walked off by the side of the school. I sat down. I thought about what I wanted to say."

Hornsby felt terrible. What if he promised him that he would be back tomorrow to watch him give the speech in front of the class but couldn't make it back to 1884? What if, just like today where he was left all alone in a closet, he would be left standing in front of a tough audience without proper support? Hornsby wondered how he could prevent this from backfiring even more to the point John W. Davis remained America's thirtieth president forever. "Go ahead," he said. "I'm listening."

"Right now?"

"Yes. Give me your speech."

"Just to you?"

"Yes. Go ahead, Calvin."

Hornsby was waiting for him to start talking about his father's business. That was, after all, what they discussed earlier in the day. Little did he expect this.

"This is a speech about my mother."

Calvin froze up. Hornsby gave him a nod to keep going.

"Two weeks ago, she was given to the Lord. She was ill. I would like to talk about how much I miss her and how she was the most important person in my life." Hornsby smiled and gave Calvin another nod of encouragement. "My mother was named Victoria. She gave the warmest hugs…" Calvin began to get choked up. "She always cooked us dinner, and she always had us in clean clothes. She always told me the Lord loves me and the Lord always believes in me. I miss her so much now."

"That was wonderful, Calvin."

Hornsby began to think of his own mother and kept replaying the words "I would like to talk about how much I miss her and how she was the most important person in my life" in his head. His own eyes became watery, but he did not let Calvin see it.

"You okay, Mr. Hornsby?"

"Yeah, yeah I'm fine. I wish I wrote a speech for my own mother. That was really nice."

"How come you didn't?"

"I guess I'm not as great at giving speeches as you are."

Hornsby kept thinking about the day in seventh grade when he returned home and his mother was nowhere to be found, not even a message or note was left. And then Mr. Wells, a good friend of his mother's, knocked on the door. "I'm afraid your mother has gone away for a while, Ethan. But I promise to find her." No one ever did, not Mr. Wells, not the detectives. *How could you abandon me, Mom? Didn't you love me?*

"Did you want me to say it to the class tomorrow?" asked Calvin.

"That's up to you. And you should know, I might not be back here. I might have another class to teach far away from here. If I am back, I look forward to spending the day with you boys. If I'm not, I want you to always remember this, I also believe in you." Calvin nodded. "Now head on home now. You have a long walk."

Calvin began to walk away. He turned. "Thanks, Mr. Hornsby. I feel better now."

Hornsby watched as the boy hit the open dirt road.

He wandered back inside, looked around, and quietly slid back out into the Upper Kakapo hallway.

He opened a laptop and did a search for Calvin Coolidge. "Oh no."

To his dismay, John W. Davis was still the thirtieth president.

7

Hornsby sat dejected at his desk, listening to both the final announcements of the day over the loudspeaker and the ruckus of the student masses exiting the building, unable to enjoy the comforts of his modern chair. Suddenly, there was a knock on the door from Mrs. Peacock's assistant. "Hi, Mr. Hornsby."

"Hi."

"Mrs. Peacock and Mr. Waters asked to meet with you. They are in Mrs. Peacock's office."

Hornsby did his best to maintain his composure and thank her with a smile, but inside, he knew what this meant. He looked around the room, taking in his last looks at the inside of an Upper Kakapo classroom. Not only had he ruined history, but he also was now about to be fired, most likely meaning that he would never have the chance to get back to 1884 to fix his mess.

Here was the even more devastating news about what happens if you get fired as a substitute teacher on Long Island—other districts would surely follow Upper Kakapo's lead, as he would be unable to obtain letters of recommendations or references. Who was he supposed to get a positive recommendation letter from, Mr. Begget in 1884?

He was doomed forever—on every level.

He could hear Mrs. Peacock's voice. "Maybe you should find another purpose for all that historical information you have locked up in your brain," she had told him. But maybe she was right all along. Maybe he was better off far away from a classroom, possibly as some city librarian or some tour guide at a museum.

He timidly dragged his feet down the hallway as he made his way into Mrs. Peacock's office. She was indeed sitting alongside Old Man Waters. But what he wasn't expecting was that Mr. Slattery and his overly confident demeanor was also in the meeting.

Hornsby's eyes made their way from Slattery to Peacock and then back to Slattery. He could hear Slattery's voice from when he was blocking him in the hallway, saying, "I'm going to share a little bit of important information with you." It was the information that Waters was making his rounds in the building. But how else would Slattery have had this information unless it had been given to him on a silver platter by Peacock? Once again, it was clear she was doing everything in her power to make sure Slattery would be the winner in this war for a full-time position. Slattery looked so confident. He must have even known this interview was coming. She probably also fed him the questions.

"Mr. Hornsby, please have a seat," said Old Man Waters. Hornsby sat down alongside Slattery. "As I'm sure you boys already know, this is a very competitive profession. Rarely does a social studies job open up on Long Island. And when it does, there's a long line out the door of qualified candidates. That's why I take it very seriously, knowing exactly who my substitute teachers are and how I can help them grow as young teachers. Unfortunately for some, I also use these opportunities to weed out those who are not worth us investing our time and resources. This career is not for everyone. And like other careers, some just will never cut it. I happily had a chance to get a look at both of you in action, and now I just wanted to follow it up with one question only."

"Just like I was ready for anything in the classroom, I'm ready for any question you may have, sir," responded Slattery.

"Well, okay then, Mr. Slattery, my only question today for both of you is, 'What have you learned so far about yourself?'"

Slattery moved his hand in front of Hornsby as if to push him out of the way. "What I learned is how much I enjoy spending my days around our youth. I've learned how much joy I get bringing smiles to their faces. You should have seen how much they laughed when I did my Lincoln versus Washington rap battle. I learned that

I have this unique ability to connect with them and to connect them to history. I also learned that I could be depended upon to get the job done! Just ask Mrs. Peacock."

"Absolutely. That is very true, Mr. Waters," Peacock added.

"And that I can make my coworkers laugh," he continued. "Camaraderie is such an important ingredient to good faculty culture. In conclusion, I have what it takes to win teacher of the year every year!"

"Nice to see how confident you are, Mr. Slattery. And may I add that I was very impressed by what I saw taking place inside your room. There was quite a bit of learning. You're obviously a natural." He paused. "What about you, Mr. Hornsby? What have you learned about yourself?"

Hornsby looked over at Peacock, who seemed to be taking great joy in this. Slattery crossed his legs and leaned back.

It was quiet. It felt like minutes went by. Waters was growing uncomfortable from the awkwardness. "Mr. Hornsby? Everything okay?"

"No, everything is not okay." Hornsby stood up and headed for the door. He thought about his future as a museum tour guide.

"But you haven't answered my question?"

"Okay, Mr. Waters. Here is what I've learned about myself. I learned that I'm finding this job to be very hard. And I'm learning how often I make mistakes, particularly with students. For example, there was a student, and get this, I already knew the outcome. I already knew how his story would end, yet I still managed to screw it up. And that really scares me because it got me to wonder what would happen when there is a student and I don't know the outcome? How many mistakes will I make then? What if next time I'm too hard on a student? When should I go easy? Or if I'm too easy on a student, when I should be firmer? Or when I should just be talking, not listening? Or I should be listening, instead of talking?" Hornsby paused. "What I'm mostly trying to say is, I've learned that I'm scared to death of letting my students down. I want to be their hero. But I'm not sure how to be that."

There was silence. It sounded as if Peacock was about to burst out in laughter, same with Slattery. "I've been doing this for near fifty years, Mr. Hornsby," said Old Man Waters. "And that might be the most truthful, thoughtful"—he looked Slattery right in the eyes—"and honest answer I've ever heard. You should know, Mr. Hornsby, even after fifty years, I feel the same way each and every day. And I still make mistakes myself, a lot of them." He took a moment to reflect. "Mr. Hornsby, your answer is the exact message that our students need to hear. Please make sure you share it with them going forward."

Going forward? Does that mean I'm not fired?

"Thank you, gentlemen, for your time. See you both back here, business as usual tomorrow."

Business as usual tomorrow?

Hornsby reached the hallway and began to make his way back to Mrs. Keptoe's room.

Mrs. Peacock came out of her office, turned the corner, and approached, sticking her mouth next to his ear. "That's the last time you will ever make me look bad, Hornsby."

Then came Slattery, the former lacrosse jock easily catching up to him. "No more Mr. Nice Guy from me, *Thorns*by. Now it's officially war." He took off in the other direction.

Hornsby entered his room to grab his coat. He had so much on his mind. He hadn't even thought about what could happen once he got back inside. Or maybe he just assumed since the day was over, he wouldn't be doing any more time traveling.

But he was now standing inside an unfamiliar den, across from an African American housemaid. She wore a black cap with white ruffles in the front and a long, puffed-out dress with a white apron. Hornsby wondered if this woman worked for the Coolidge family, and he questioned where Calvin could be.

"Mr. Hornsby?" she asked with a Midwestern drawl.

Hornsby found the tidy one-window den rather charming. Over the fireplace was the magnificent head of a moose, and there were books lined up inside a large case. He placed his hand on the earth-toned upholstered chair to feel the homemade fabric, and he examined the small pipe and ashtray on the wooden table. But, boy, the musty smell of the house—it was like being hit with the odor of a thousand wet socks at once. He walked over to the grand oil painting of a large family on the far wall to see if Calvin was in it. But he wasn't one of them. "Yes, I'm Mr. Hornsby."

Hornsby knew from his last travel that flying back at least a century was possible. Now he began to wonder if he had traveled back to an even earlier time period and if this woman was a slave.

"Benjamin is out back."

"Ah yes, Benjamin. Who is Benjamin?"

"You'll be tutoring him."

"Exactly, just as I'd planned. Tutoring Benjamin." Hornsby looked around. He needed to locate something with a date on it. There was a newspaper on the table next to the ashtray and pipe. It took a moment for Hornsby's eyes to adjust to the lack of light without the fireplace or the lamps nailed to the walls being lit. "May I?"

The woman nodded.

It was the *Indianapolis Times*, and it was stamped with the date May 10, 1844. Hornsby fell into the snug chair. Reality set in. He was in an even earlier year than before—forty years earlier.

"Mr. Hornsby?" the housemaid tried to get his attention. But Hornsby was busy trying to add up what this Benjamin could possibly have to do with an unborn Calvin. "Mr. Hornsby?" she asked again.

"I'm sorry, I never asked your name?"

"My name is Charlotte."

"And do you live here also?"

"I do."

"Are you by yourself or with family?"

"My boy lives here with me."

Hornsby knew from the newspaper that they were in Indiana. He also knew that Indiana was a free state in 1844 but largely unfriendly to blacks. "What's your son's name?"

"Jeremiah."

"That's a very nice name."

"Thank you, Mr. Hornsby."

"And you said Benjamin is where?"

"Out back. Last I saw him, he was in the barn." It felt as if Charlotte was warming up to Mr. Hornsby's kindness. She added, "You should know, you're the third tutor this month."

"Are there other boys and girls or just Benjamin?"

"Yes, sir. There are others. But them at school." Hornsby took another look at the family in the painting.

"Well, thank you, Ms. Charlotte." Hornsby made sure to walk over and gently shake her hand. She didn't appear used to that.

He then walked out of the single-floor farmhouse, which was up on a hill overlooking pasture and woods. There were narrow strips of gardens, and plump cows were out in the field grazing. He saw a small cottage behind the farmhouse and guessed it was where Charlotte and Jeremiah lived. To the left was a barn with a team of gorgeous stallions in front, a sure sign of wealth. Beyond it were fenced in goats and sheep, and beyond them was a chicken coup. A narrow stream seemed to split the landscape into two, offering the most pleasant sound of running water. He knelt down by it and reached his open palms into the cold water, cupping himself a refreshing sip. He then made his way over to pet the horses. The winds picked up, and there was a rattle from whatever creaky old boards and rusty nails were holding the barn together.

Hornsby entered the barn and immediately gagged from the grotesque combination of animal urine and manure, combined with the dirty air from dust, spiderwebs, straw, and hay. He didn't notice the empty feed bucket by his feet and accidentally kicked it hard, startling the horses. He couldn't escape the smell, as there were even more feed buckets to his left and a moldy, broken-down wagon up on stilts.

Then out from behind the wagon came a young boy about ten years old, with filthy cheeks and messy brown hair, wearing a wrinkled tan wool shirt and overalls. "Hi, Ben. My name is Mr. Hornsby."

"Oh good, someone else to play soldiers and Indians with me."

"I would love to play soldiers and Indians with you."

"Okay, you're the Indian."

38

It made sense now why Ben needed a tutor while the rest of the children were at school and why he was his third tutor this month.

Benjamin picked up a rifle and aimed it right at Hornsby. "Die, Indian."

He fired.

8

Hornsby dove behind haystacks as a bullet came flying past. "Benjamin, stop!"

"Indian in the barn!" Ben screamed as he reloaded and cocked the rifle. "We must kill all of them!"

"No!" cried Hornsby, this time diving behind the wagon, his glasses flying from his head. "Put down the rifle!"

All of a sudden, young Ben did stop. "Okay, I'll be the Indian now."

"Nooo, you will *not*. We're done with this game." Hornsby picked up his glasses and approached to take away the rifle, but Ben was already over in the corner of the barn, grabbing what looked like an authentic set of native bow and arrows. Like an expert, he quickly cocked an arrow. Hornsby reacted quickly enough to dive again behind the same haystacks. "Stop it, Ben! Stop it now!"

"I will not!"

Ben cocked another arrow.

Hornsby never knew he had this type of courage in him. But it was time to stand up to this kid. He walked speedily at the boy with his finger pointed. With ferocity on his face and rage in his voice, he roared, "Yes, you will, young man! Put the weapon down now!"

Young Ben met his match. Hornsby grabbed the bow out of his hands and threw it in the corner. He stuck his finger in Ben's face. "Now you listen to me, young man. I'm in charge here. Everything I tell you to do, you will listen to me. If you don't, there will be *real* Indians who will be coming to kill us. Do you understand?"

"Yes."

"What? I couldn't hear you?"

"Yes."

"Yes, what?"

"Yes, sir."

"Now go over to that haystack and sit your behind down. And do not move until I tell you."

"All right."

"All right, what?"

"All right, sir."

It was obvious to Hornsby that the lessons Ben was going to need had nothing to do with academics. "Actually, I can't handle the smell in this barn. Why don't we go outside for some fresh air? And maybe you can tell me about those two beautiful horses out there."

Ben perked up. "This is Trigger." Hornsby moved his hand across the muscular silky smooth shoulder of the stallion. "I love to ride him."

"You get to ride such a big horse?"

"Yes, sir, I do. He's a joy. Got my own leather saddle too."

"And who is this?"

"This is Chestnut. He's Pa's pride and joy. Real fast. But hard to unwind."

Hornsby petted Chestnut right between the eyes. "Does your pa let you ride him also?"

"No. He doesn't think I'm ready. Pa says that he gets too mad."

"Then I'll make you a deal," Hornsby said. "You do everything I tell you to do from here on out, and I'll talk to your pa about letting you have a go with Chestnut."

"Really?"

"Yes. Let's start with you telling me more about yourself, Ben. What's your last name?"

"Harrison. My last name is Harrison."

Hornsby froze. The only Benjamin Harrison he knew of was the twenty-third president from 1889 to 1893. "I'll be right back." Hornsby walked back over to look at the farmhouse again. He did recall reading that even though the Harrison's were a family of aristocrats, settling in Virginia as early as the 1600s in Jamestown, that

Benjamin's father did maintain a simple farming life. There was only one more question for him to ask that would certify if this was *that* Benjamin Harrison. "Was your grandfather President William Henry Harrison?"

"Yes, sir."

Oh my god, this is that Benjamin Harrison.

Benjamin and his grandfather, William Henry Harrison, had two claims to fame. One, they were the only grandfather/grandson pair to become presidents. Two, William Henry had the shortest tenure in history as president, as he died right after his first month in office. His wife, Benjamin's grandmother, never even had the chance to finish packing for Washington before receiving the news. Some blamed his long inauguration speech in the rain. But Hornsby wasn't ready for this.

"My pa says Grandpa was poisoned."

Hornsby's eyes shot out of their sockets. "Poisoned?"

"Uh-huh."

"Did he say by whom?"

"His enemies, of course. Pa says we all got 'em."

Hornsby thought about Slattery. "He's right about that."

Hornsby was now itching to get on a computer to do some research into Benjamin's grandpa's cause of death. But this was all just so crazy. First, he was sitting alongside a twelve-year-old Calvin Coolidge and now, a ten-year-old Benjamin Harrison. Who was next? And what about Calvin's fate? How could he get back to 1884 to fix that course of history? And was there some link between Harrison and Coolidge that he never knew about? There was obviously something much bigger going on here than he could even imagine.

Hornsby could immediately tell this trip into 1844 was going to be far different than his last escapade. Benjamin was not some son of an ordinary merchant. Not only was Grandpa Harrison a president of the United States, but his great-grandfather was also a signer of the Declaration of Independence. No wonder Benjamin was rebelling. He had all the pressure of restoring the famous Harrison name in politics, prestige, and power bestowed upon him.

This was also going to be different because this was the era of westward expansion, and from what Hornsby knew about Grandpa William Henry Harrison, he was hailed as a war hero for leading successful military victories against Indians even before he became president. He was one of many who helped open up the Northwest Territory for white settlers. No wonder Ben thought a game of shooting Indians was fun.

"Do you have friends that you play around with?" Ben shrugged his shoulders. "Well, there must be other boys from around town that would love to play soldiers and Indians with you?" Ben wouldn't answer. Hornsby looked at the small cottage where Charlotte and Jeremiah lived. "What about Jeremiah, do you play with him?"

Suddenly, Ben became even more uncomfortable. He put his head down. "No, sir."

"Would you want to play with him?"

But Ben wouldn't say. Hornsby began to wonder.

Charlotte stepped outside and looked over from the front of the farmhouse, as she placed laundry on clotheslines. Hornsby noticed just about all the clothes were soft colors, but then there was this ultra-red shirt that hung on the very end.

"Wait right here, Ben," Hornsby said. He walked over to Charlotte. "Ms. Charlotte, does Ben not have any friends to play with?"

"He got friends."

"Oh, okay, because when I asked him about it, he seemed to not want to talk about it. Did something happen?"

"No, Mr. Hornsby. Everything fine."

Hornsby reflected on the year 1844 and the racial division in the nation, even in a northern state like Indiana. "Does your son Jeremiah play with Ben?"

But Charlotte didn't care for that question. "You keep my son outta your business, Mr. Hornsby." She looked over at Ben. "And outta his." Hornsby noticed that she was extra securing the ultra-red shirt on the clothesline as the wind picked up.

"I promise to respect your wishes, Ms. Charlotte. Thank you for your help." Hornsby watched as she walked back inside the farmhouse.

As Hornsby walked back to Ben, out of nowhere, he heard a female voice. "Watch out for the Loyalists." But there was no one around, and it definitely was not Charlotte. Hornsby was confused. Where did this voice come from? Was it his conscience talking to him? And who are the Loyalists? Hornsby looked around a second time. Ben began to walk away toward the house. "Where are you going, Ben?"

"To my room."

"Did I say you could leave?"

"I don't need your permission."

"Yes, you do, your parents put me in charge."

"Ma will just fire you like the others."

"What about getting to ride Chestnut? I promised you I would talk to your pa."

"Don't need it. Next year, I'll be old enough."

"I can tell something's bothering you, Ben. We should talk about it." But Ben just kept walking away. "Okay then, you've left me no choice." Ben turned, as he had to see what Mr. Hornsby was doing. "Do you know what I do when I feel sad?" Hornsby busted out into a dance.

"No?"

"Renegade, renegade, go…go…come on, Ben, TikTok, baby, go…go…look at this, Ben, move your arms with me…renegade, renegade…" Ben looked at Hornsby's waist as his belly was flopping around. "Renegade, renegade, go…go…move your arms like this, Ben. Let's go!"

"What are you doing, Mr. Hornsby?"

"It's your birthday. We gon' party like it's yo birthday."

"It's my birthday?"

"Look, Ben, now I'm moving my hips like I just don't care."

"You don't care?"

"Nope."

"Why not?"

"Because music's so exciting. I can't fight it. I can't hide it."

"It is?"

"Look, now I've got my hands in the air because I just don't care. You can do it too. Put those hands in the air." Ben began to follow along. "Now wave 'em like you just don't care. And get those hips moving."

"Like this?"

"Watch me. I'm waving my arms and moving my hips because we just don't care."

"Is this right?"

"Sure is. Now I want to hear you say it, 'I just don't care.'"

"I just don't care."

"Now let's slow it down, moving our bodies even slower…okay, let's let it all go." Hornsby stopped. He was dripping in sweat. "Hey, is that a smile I see?" Ben was still moving his hips around, waving his arms. "I can't hear you?"

"I just don't care."

"What?"

"I just don't care."

"Can't hear you?"

"I just don't care!" Ben screamed. Charlotte peeked her head out from the front door. Hornsby waved that everything was okay.

"Am I a renegade yet?"

"You sure are. And I want you to always remember this, whenever you feel sad, you raise those arms, you shake those hips, and you scream it out, okay?"

"Yes, sir."

"The Loyalists are near." There was that female voice a second time. Hornsby looked around again, but there was no one there.

Who was the voice referring to? The only Loyalists Hornsby knew of were the colonists who lived during the era of the thirteen colonies, who remained loyal to England rather than join the American Revolution for independence. Many were afraid of what the king would do to them if they were disloyal. Others just wanted the colonies to remain under England's control. But now he was in 1844. There were already twenty-six states by this time. What could this time period possibly have to do with people who lived all the way back then? From Calvin's time period then to Benjamin's and now to the American Revolution? What did any of this have in common?

Wait a minute, Hornsby thought. The last time he time traveled, he was outside with Calvin. And when he walked back into the classroom, Mrs. Peacock was there with the Upper Kakapo students. She proved, by entering, she could interfere with his journey. Maybe he was somehow hearing the voice of a history teacher who was close by, possibly inside his classroom. Was Mrs. Keptoe back to teaching a lesson?

Ben was still waving his arms in the air. "Wave 'em like I just don't care."

Hornsby knelt down on his right knee. "I had fun, Ben. But I need to go now for the day, okay. But I promise I'll be back soon."

"Why do you have to go?"

"Oh, so now you don't want me to leave?"

Ben began to move his hips around. "Am I doing good? Do I not care?"

"You're doing great pal. But I still gotta go."

"Okay, bye, Mr. Hornsby."

Hornsby took another look at the farmhouse, thinking about his conversation with Charlotte. He watched as the ultra-red shirt blew in the wind. "I want you to know, you can always trust me, Ben." Ben nodded. "Even with a big secret." Ben nodded again. Hornsby patted him on the head and stood up. "I hope to see you again soon."

Hornsby rushed inside to his point of entrance, the den, and crossed along into a hallway, which brought him back to the hallway of Upper Kakapo. He looked inside the empty classroom. Not only were there no students but also there were no teachers either.

He checked the time. It was nearing the dinner hour. Everyone was gone for the day.

9

Completely exhausted and utterly confused after such a strange long day, Hornsby finally arrived at his home. As usual, he entered to piles of dust, worn furniture, an empty refrigerator, and painful memories of his mother. And there were historical books everywhere—in the bathroom, in the laundry room, on the staircase, even in the pantry. He dropped his bag on the floor and plopped down on the couch. He could feel tightness in his back from all the dancing, yet his mind was still running sprints.

Somewhere in all those piles was the all-everything-book about President Benjamin Harrison, and Hornsby knew he needed to read up quickly before he screwed up Ben's future, the way he did Calvin's.

From the kitchen to the laundry room to the staircase, he looked everywhere before his eyes found their way to a photo of him and his mom on a small table in the living room. He walked over and used his fingers to wipe away some dust from the glass before taking it in his hand as he sat down against the wall. He took a moment to observe all the loneliness. "Why did you leave me, Mom?"

But then he noticed one of his books had somehow gotten wedged behind a large bookcase to his right. He tried to slide his hand through to reach it, but it wouldn't fit. He got up and slid the heavy bookcase out. Nope, not the Harrison book, just another one of his many Civil War ones. But then he noticed a deep hole in the wall. "Oh great, now another thing I need to fix in this darn house." He ran around to the other side of the wall and into his bedroom to see if the hole extended through to the other side. But the wall on that side was fine. This meant, there must be space in between the rooms. He peeled away a larger piece of drywall and stuck his head through. Not only was there a hidden space between the walls, but it also appeared large enough to be a closet. It also appeared like there might be stuff in there. He began to peel away even more of the wall. He even kicked at it as the mess piled up. Finally, he was able to wedge his body into the opening and flashed light from his phone. "What in the world?"

He shined his light all around the hidden closet, revealing not only objects but also cobwebs and the skeleton of a dead mouse. After closer inspection, he found an oil painting on the floor and a small shelf full of stuff to his left. He wiped away dirt and grime, revealing an old leather book, a dress, and a pair of handmade, primitive-looking shoes. "Holy cow." He then zoomed his light on the oil painting for a better look. It was a portrait of a woman from an era ago, but unfortunately, the mouse must have taken a bite out of it. A large piece of her face was missing.

He carried out the items and placed them on the kitchen table. First, he focused on the leather book, which was hand-bound by a string. He opened to the first page and saw the name, written in script, Jane Pierce. He had to sit down once seeing the year was 1586. And yet the more he cleaned it up, the more surprised he was by its good condition. The paper inside had not yet lost its color. There was very little wear along the edges, and none of the ink faded. Was it a fake? And why was it snuggled away in his house? Did his mother even know about this secret closet?

He read on. The first few entries were about this woman's journey with her husband from England to their new American colony. Then there were pages devoted to settlement, and she even wrote about them trying to grow tobacco. He wondered if this was the woman in the painting. But why would anyone put this much attention and detail into a fake document? And the more he examined the writing, the more he wondered why the handwriting resembled his mother's. And what was with the dress and shoes?

He took a soapy wet cloth and wiped away as much dust as he could to bring the painting back to life. The woman was wearing her black hair in a bun and was wearing this exact dress that was now on his table. Was this Jane Pierce who owned the journal? He wondered if an expert could repair the piece of her face that was missing.

Hornsby knew who to call for answers. Jim Wells was not only his mother's old friend, who led the search for her, but he was also the top antique dealer in town. Wells had not only purchased this house as an investment property, allowing Hornsby to live here, but he was also granted custody, allowing him to avoid foster homes. Hornsby worked at his shop over the summer and thought of him like an uncle.

"Ethan, is everything okay?"

"Are you still at the shop?"

"Was just about to close up for the night. What's up?"

"Don't leave just yet. I have something I need you to see right away."

*****

Jim Wells wasn't even as tall as the antique coat rack that stood by the entrance to his store. He wore thick bifocal glasses and walked with a slight limp to his right leg, but, boy, for an older fellow, Hornsby always thought the man was in serious physical shape. He came out from behind the glass counter which featured everything from rare baseball cards to priceless Tiffany glasswork and collectible GI Joe action figures. The bones in Hornsby's hand were almost crunched into pieces by Well's handshake. "What do we have here?"

"They were in the house, hidden in some secret closet."

"Our house has a secret closet?"

"It does, behind the living room wall. Do you know when it would have been built?"

"Must go back to the original owners before your mom bought it. The house goes as far back as the late 1960s."

"Do you think Mom would have known about it?"

"She certainly never said anything to me."

"Take a look at the first page. It says it's from 1586."

Wells turned the pages but seemed to have the same initial reaction as Hornsby did. If the journal was over four hundred years old, why didn't it look it? He took out his small magnifying glass and examined it closer. He then went into the back and came out with another book. "This is a book from that era and an example of what proper aging would do to paper after centuries. I don't think your journal is real."

"What about the dress and shoes?"

"Well, they definitely reflect the style of that era. I can't rule them out until I have one of my experts examine them, but given that they are alongside a fake document, I wouldn't get my hopes up. Give me a week, okay?"

"Okay, Mr. Wells, but they must have been important to someone, why else hide them?" Hornsby pointed at a page. "And why put so much detail into each entry? That's a lot of work."

"I've seen it all. You would be surprised by what lengths people would go to to pass off fakes as authentic. There's quite a bit of money to be made in antiquities."

Hornsby turned the pages again. He hadn't noticed before. "Hmmm, I wonder why some pages in the back are torn out."

Wells examined it. "Just another missing piece to our puzzle. Let's take it one step at a time, okay? Let my experts examine the dress and the shoes, and then we can work to figure out who was this Jane Pierce."

"Okay, thank you, Mr. Wells." Hornsby took one last look inside the journal. "It's weird. The handwriting looks just like my mom's."

"I doubt your mother would have spent her days creating forgeries." Wells looked closer at Hornsby's eyes. "Have you been getting enough rest, Ethan?"

Hornsby took a deep breath. He was still feeling the pinch in his back from all the dancing with Ben. "You wouldn't believe that this isn't even the craziest thing to happen to me today."

*****

Jim Wells watched Hornsby exit. He picked up his phone to make a call. "He was just here."

"And?" asked the deep voice.

"He had the journal and clothes."

"But you promised his mother destroyed the evidence."

"She swore to me she did. But it's why I bought the house, just in case. God forbid any of it got into the wrong hands."

"We should assume there's even more in there."

"He didn't have the painting."

"Then let's hope he never sees it."

"When the time is right, I'll take a closer look around the house."

"The time is now, Jim," responded the deep voice.

"No," said Wells as he continued to think about Hornsby. "Round up the team. There are more pressing issues to discuss."

10

The next morning, Hornsby was a motormouth, as he walked with Rosie into the school, trying to catch her up on his adventure into 1844 and the secret closet. She stayed by his side as he received his daily assignment. Today, he was covering for a science teacher, and they wondered if the same thing would happen to him in this new room. Rosie entered first, just in case. "Maybe the journal was brought back by another time traveler, and that's why it's not as old as it should be?"

"I considered that possibility," said Hornsby, "but then I remembered when you tried to bring back one of the Bibles."

"Oh yeah, it won't let you."

"And get this, when I was back in 1844, out of nowhere, came this woman's voice."

"Maybe it was Peacock? That woman would find a way to haunt us from anywhere," Rosie joked as she sat down.

"It didn't sound evil enough to be her." Hornsby laughed.

"Do you think maybe you imagined it?"

"I wish I could say I imagined the whole day." Hornsby wiped the sweat from his brow. "Look at me. The day hasn't even begun, and I'm already nervously sweating like a pig."

"What are you gonna do if you keep hearing this voice?"

"Try to figure out who these Loyalists are, I guess. But I'll admit, it sounds really scary and stuff being warned to watch out for them."

Rosie could see it in his eyes that Hornsby hadn't slept all night. "I can't imagine what you are going through right now, Ethan. But if it makes you feel any better, when I started as a sub, I always felt like I was being pulled in a million directions."

"Yeah, but at least you were in the room and could teach. Being a teacher here was all I ever dreamed of, and right as I get my chance, this happens. I want to be able to teach the kids walking in here, not kids from the past."

Rosie thought it over. "Maybe you *are* in the room."

"I am?"

"Like when I saw a fake version of you sit down at the desk and pick up a book to read."

"Yeah, but when Peacock entered my room, she accused me of leaving my kids alone, which means she didn't see this fake me." Hornsby paused. "I'm not sure which scenario is making me more nervous."

"Just keep in mind, Ethan, you already leaped over the toughest hurdle. Old Man Waters really likes you."

"He won't like me for long if these science students are all alone playing with hazardous chemicals and lab equipment."

"The odds of a very busy superintendent spending any more of his precious time worrying about observing you or any other sub is pretty slim. So the coast will be clear for a while." Rosie could tell there was something else just eating away at Hornsby. "What else is worrying you, Ethan?"

Hornsby sat down. "Have you ever heard of the Roaring Twenties?"

"No. What is it like a bunch of twenty-dollar bills screaming out loud or something?" She laughed.

"No. It was an expression that came from the decade of the 1920s when there was economic prosperity and strength."

"I've never heard it before."

"That's because Calvin Coolidge never became president."

Rosie responded, "I thought the Great Depression took place during the 1920s."

"All the way through the 1930s?"

"Yeah."

"But that's only the way history's written now because I screwed up Calvin Coolidge's life somehow. Before I traveled, the Great Depression, a time of economic hardship and misfortune for most Americans, didn't technically start until after Calvin was out of office, and it really didn't get bad for people until the 1930s."

"So you think you caused an extension of the worst economic time in America?"

"I know I did. And think about how many more people must have gotten hurt because of me."

"I'm sorry, Ethan, but this isn't adding up. You couldn't have completely changed the trajectory of this country in just one day."

"Maybe Calvin was really hurt by having to wait in the closet because I never showed up?"

"Could that be?"

"I don't know. But I wish I knew how to control this to get back to him and fix whatever I did wrong. And what if I let Ben down next?"

"There's something much bigger going on here, Ethan, and somehow, you innocently wound up stuck right in the middle of it." Rosie paused. "And I've suddenly become fascinated by history. After you texted me, I looked up Benjamin Harrison last night. Imagine that"—Rosie smiled—"me looking up ex-presidents."

"I can't."

"Did you know he was the first president to have his voice recorded? It was from 1889, and it's on YouTube. It's so neat to hear him."

"No, I didn't. That is neat. Well, I did some digging around online myself about Grandpa William Henry Harrison possibly being poisoned. And I think their family was on to something. Historians have always accepted the autopsy from Harrison's doctor that it was pneumonia of the right lung, but now some investigators believe his death was caused by a smelly marsh that was near the White House. There was no sewer system back then. So some of the human waste would overflow onto the White House grounds. New theories are that bacteria may have contaminated his water supply."

"Then, in a way, it was poison."

"Yes. But it was certainly not murder. Just possibly a victim of primitive technology. Two other presidents from that era also got sick, though they survived."

The opening morning bell rang. That meant the students were on their way into the building from their busses. "Well, I gotta get to the library. Hopefully, if you travel, fake you will be at your desk to at least look the part."

"If I do travel again, I just wish I knew what to do."

"Just be yourself."

Hornsby started dancing. "Like when I did the renegade song with Ben?"

Rosie's mouth dropped. "No, you didn't."

"Oh yes, I did. Come on, Rosie, get those arms moving...renegade, renegade, go...go..."

Rosie laughed out loud. "What I would have given to have witnessed that." She started dancing. "And I take it back. Do not be yourself."

Hornsby then placed his hand up to his ear. "Do you hear something? I think it's the sounds of the..." Hornsby began to dance the Macarena. "How about this one for today's lesson?"

"I think you doing the Macarena will be your best defense against the Loyalists as they will instantly run for the hills."

"Very cute, Rosie."

Rosie began to exit but turned back at the doorway. "Try not to have too much fun without me."

"Do you think I should leave my phone, wallet, jacket, and stuff hung up in the hallway closet? The kids in Calvin's class were asking about the iPhone."

"That's probably best. God forbid anything modern gets into the wrong hands back then. I would think kids from the 1800s doing TikTok dances will be damaging enough to civilization." Rosie laughed.

"Oh, and Rosie?"

"Yeah?"

"Thanks."

*****

Mr. Slattery watched as Hornsby placed his iPhone, wallet, and keys in his jacket pocket before hanging it up in the hallway closet. He covertly made his way over, and before the phone locked, he reached in and took it from the coat.

"Old Man Waters won't be fond of you for long, *Thorn*sby," he said, taking off down the hallway.

11

Hornsby found Ben at the edge of the woods with an ax, trying to chop at a pile of lumber. "Hi, Ben."

"Mr. Hornsby, you came back!"

"Here I am!"

"Look." Ben started shaking his hips. "Shake 'em like you just don't care."

Hornsby moved his hips in unison.

"I'm waving my arms, Mr. Hornsby."

"Great job again, Ben." Hornsby also waved his arms in the air. Then he motioned for Ben to sit down on one of the logs. "What's your pa having you do down here?"

"He wanted me to gather up wood chips for the barn."

"Doesn't look like that's what you're doing."

"Pa ain't here."

"But he's expecting that you'll follow his orders. And I don't think he wants you swinging that heavy ax."

"Do it all the time."

"Not well, I see."

"So?"

"What happened to saying the word 'sir?'"

Ben turned away. "Maybe you should just leave again."

"Are you sure that's what you want?"

"I reckon it is."

This time, Hornsby felt too beat up to dance and too exhausted to fight. He never wanted to be in 1844 in the first place. And maybe it was best for him to just leave before he did any more damage to

America's story. He began to walk up the hill. But then he peeked back, seeing a child who he knew was hurting badly inside.

He headed back down to Ben. "It's a shame I have to leave. I was planning to give out star stickers to all my best listeners."

"What's a star sticker?"

"It's a big star that will stick to your shirt. It shows everyone, and I mean *everyone*, who the star listeners are."

"Can I have one?"

Hornsby knelt down on his right knee once again. "I'm going to make you a promise, the next time we see each other, I will have one of those stars for you. Cross my heart, okay?"

"Yes, sir."

"But remember, only the star listeners get one. And that means, doing what you're told even if you don't want to." Hornsby sat down next to Ben on the log. "I'm sure it's really tough being a Harrison. Your great-grandpa signed the Declaration of Independence, and your grandpa was president. That's some important legacy to live up to."

"But I'm gonna just be a farmer like Pa."

Hornsby noticed up on the clothesline. All the clothes had been removed, but the ultra-red shirt was still hanging. "Why do you want to be a farmer?"

"To stay here all my life and ride Trigger and Chestnut."

"Your pa loves this land, doesn't he?"

"Yes, sir."

"He takes good care of it."

"Sure does."

Hornsby pointed at the woods. "Scary what's happening across the country."

"What do you mean?"

"Whole forests being cut down to build homes. Soon we'll keep moving west, just like your grandpa wanted, but animals like the bison will be killed to near extinction. Other animals, too, like the beaver."

"What's that mean, extinction?"

"It means that these animals will disappear from Earth for good. No more bison."

"For good? Do people know this?"

"If they do know, they aren't very concerned with it. It's going to take a leader to come up with a plan to save our natural world. Wouldn't your pa want to save this simple way of life?"

"He does."

"Then what should we do? We need to still cut down trees for wood. So will others. And people are always going to need animals to eat and for clothes." Ben shook his head that he didn't have an answer. "Well, I want you to pretend that your pa became president of the United States and he had to come up with a solution. What would he do?"

"Don't know."

"Think about it."

"I reckon he'd say we should allow people to cut down some trees but not all."

"Preserve some areas?"

"Yes, sir."

"I think that's a great plan, and you're gonna follow through on it when you get older."

"I am?"

"You are. I believe in you, Ben. But caring about the land and riding your horses isn't the only reason why you want to stay here and live on this farm, is it?" Ben shifted his body away. Hornsby looked again at the ultra-red shirt on the clothesline. He looked over at the pile of chopped wood and the ax. Hornsby headed into the woods, pushing branches aside until he came upon a cutout, an empty space of land in between the trees. On the ground was a book, *A Pretty Little Pocket*, which Hornsby knew was one of the first children's books ever published. He examined it. Ben entered the cutout. "So this is the real reason why you come down here to chop wood."

"I like to come here and read."

Hornsby continued to think about Charlotte and the ultra-red shirt. "Do you remember when I told you I could be trusted with a secret?"

"Yes, sir."

"Even a big one?"

"Yes."

"That time is now, Ben. Why don't you tell me what's really going on here?" But Ben looked away. "This is where you meet Jeremiah, isn't it?" Ben wouldn't answer. Hornsby looked again at the book. He thought about how Ben was going to grow up as America's finest gentleman, the handsome, caring Benjamin Harrison, who would fight politically for blacks to have rights such as an education. "Are you teaching him to read?" Ben put his head down. "Now you pick your head up with pride, Benjamin Harrison. I'm so proud of you." It was as if Ben had never heard those words before, and he became emotional. Hornsby understood loud and clear why Ben has become defiant and angry. He's been sneaking around his parents just to keep his friendship with Jeremiah alive. "The red shirt is on the clothesline. That's your warning from Charlotte that your ma is close, isn't it?"

"Please, Mr. Hornsby, if Ma finds out, she threatened to fire Charlotte, and that would mean Jeremiah would have to move away."

"I promised you, your secret is safe with me." Ben nodded his head. "But let's talk about how you're feeling inside." Hornsby led Ben back out to the logs, and they sat down. "What can a child do if he doesn't agree with his parents' views?"

"Don't know, Mr. Hornsby."

"It's a difficult situation. While you're young, you *must* respect your parent's rules and wishes. But as you grow older, and you move out on your own, you can become who you want to become. My advice for you, Ben, is to remember all these moments and then use all this built-up emotion. When you're an adult, think back to your secret friendship with Jeremiah and fight to make sure no other child has to go through that. Children should never be kept from playing together just because their skin is a different color."

"What if Ma and Pa don't agree with what I do as an adult?"

"You must always show your parents respect. But be prepared. They may disagree with your choices."

"But what if I want them to agree with my choices?"

"Every boy and girl grow up hoping to make their parents proud of them. It's natural to want them to think the way you do, but the only thing you can control is to be the best person you can be. They may not agree with everything you stand for, but if you're a good person who does the right thing for others, they will be proud and respect you back."

"What if I don't know what the right thing is?"

"Every person asks that same question. But you're a Harrison. What you should do is identify the good qualities of your pa and grandpa then follow the good, and more good will come. We already talked about what your pa would do to save the forests, right?"

"Yes, sir."

"And that can be half of who you become. But the other half can be who your grandpa was."

"But my grandpa would've never approved of my friendship with Jeremiah."

"What's your pa told you about him?"

"Pa said he became president because his soldiers killed Chief Tecumseh."

"That's right. Many, many Indians were killed in battles as were his soldiers. But that's not a game, Ben, like the one we played. That's real. How do you feel about people dying?"

"Not good, I reckon."

"How do you feel about Indians?"

"Pa says they're savages."

"But what if you can make a friendship with an Indian boy, just like you and Jeremiah?"

"That would be better."

"You're gonna try to help them, Ben, when you get older."

"I will?"

"You sure will. What else did your pa say about your grandpa?"

"Pa says he advanced the country."

"Well, that'll be your other half. Here's what we're gonna do. Stand up." Ben listened. "Now I'm gonna bring you *two* star stickers for being such a good listener."

"Really?"

"Your grandpa understood that great leaders fight for what they believe in, regardless of who they have to argue or debate with. And this will be your other half." Ben nodded. "Half of you will be like your pa and take care of nature, and the other half will be like grandpa, speaking up to advance the nation." Hornsby thought about how Ben would become a brigadier general for the North in the Civil War before embarking on his political career. "I can't promise that you won't have to see men die. But you can also fight for the ones who'll live so that they have a better life. Just like your grandpa tried to advance the country, so will you."

Ben seemed happy to help. "Yes, sir." Then he asked, "Can I give Jeremiah a star when he does good on his reading?"

"I think that's a wonderful idea. And just in case I'm not around, you can always carve out wood chips to look like stars."

"Yes, sir."

A woman with her hair back in a bun, wearing a sky-blue colonial-style dress with a high neckline that hung down to her shoes descended down the hill. Hornsby approached to meet her halfway. "Hello, Mr. Hornsby, I'm Mrs. Harrison."

Hornsby shook her hand. "Hello, ma'am. You and I haven't had the chance to meet yet. It's my pleasure."

Mrs. Harrison examined Hornby's clothing. "And what is it you two are doing today?"

Hornsby turned to look back at Ben, who was still sitting on the log, "Oh, just getting to know each other."

"But you are aware there are rules in this house that we follow?"

"I assumed there was. And I like rules, big fan of 'em."

"Mr. Hornsby, the good Lord set rules in place for a reason. And he created this world for my son to be the lawyer. Not that boy, Jeremiah."

"I guess I'm not sure of what you mean?"

"Charlotte is a loyal servant of our family, has been for many years. She came to me and told me that you were asking if our boys played together?"

Actually, Charlotte has been betraying you and helps the boys hide their friendship. "It was my first day. I was just trying to learn more about your son. By the way, you should be so proud of him and who he's going to become."

"Mr. Hornsby, I'm not taking a liking to your tone, in my home, no less."

Hornsby put his head down. "I don't mean to show you any disrespect, ma'am."

"Mr. Hornsby, my husband and I could have settled anywhere in this growing country. We have roots in Ohio and Virginia. We chose to build our farm in a free state for a good reason. My husband stands behind abolitionists." She raised her voice. "But that doesn't mean that boy in there is going to get the same opportunities as my son." Mrs. Harrison examined Hornsby's peculiar suit and shoes once again. "I don't recall seeing you around this town before."

"I'm not from here."

"Oh? Then what brings you to our little town?"

"I was sent here."

"From what I see, you were not sent as God set it."

Suddenly Ben approached. "I can hear you, Ma, and you're wrong. Jeremiah should have the same opportunities."

Oh no, what did I cause?

Mrs. Harrison bugged out. "You get to your room right now, Benjamin, you hear me?" Ben walked up the hill. "And don't you come out until I get there." Mrs. Harrison turned her anger toward Hornsby, "You've been fill-in my son's head with that?"

"No...well...yes, sort of... I mean, I emphasized to be respect-ful and to follow your rules and wishes. But also, that when he gets older, he should stand up for what he believes in. I pray you'll be more understanding when he defends his efforts."

"But there are plenty of other children around town he can play with."

"You mean other *white* children?"

"It's because I'm not a man that you aren't respecting my wishes?"

"It has nothing to do with you being a woman, Mrs. Harrison. It's that your son Benjamin is going to grow up in a far different country than you and I are used to. You and I both know a war with the South is inevitable."

"My husband would agree."

"That son of yours, he's going to be right at an age to go off and fight in it. But at some point—and you know the day is coming, Mrs. Harrison—all blacks will be set free across our lands. And they're going to need strong voices of support."

Mrs. Harrison just continued to examine Hornsby's every detail. "There's an evil about you, Mr. Hornsby. You're from somewhere far away. I don't know where, but it's a place maybe you should take your evil ways back to." Mrs. Harrison adjusted her dress to remain proper. "Mr. Harrison will be back from Indianapolis soon. May the good Lord watch over us. Perhaps his voice will be stronger than mine."

Suddenly, there was that faint whisper in Hornsby's ear again. And once again, it was the voice of a woman. "The Loyalists are near." His heart stopped. He looked around, but there was no one else there. "I think it's time you left for the day, Mr. Hornsby."

Hornsby knew he needed to race right back away from the Loyalists. "That, we can agree upon."

He began to walk back up to the house. "But the road is that way." Mrs. Harrison pointed.

"I just gotta get my things." Hornsby entered the home and quickly made his way to Ben's room. He heard crying. But he also heard Mrs. Harrison's footsteps approaching. He stepped back through the portal.

Immediately, he was standing inside Upper Kakapo.

Some students were doing a ditto, others were just talking to each other, and a few were on their phones playing games. But there were no adults anywhere in the vicinity. Where was this voice coming from? And had the students been left alone while he was away, or had the alternate version of him been sitting at the desk?

Hornsby, remaining out in the hallway, called on the kid who looked like the most aware of the bunch and gestured her out into the hall. He pointed at the class. "Clearly, I can't get all of them to do their work. Got any advice for a new teacher? Maybe an idea that other teachers have tried and it worked to motivate them?"

The young girl thought it over. "Candy always works."

"Candy, right. Doctors have been wrong all along. Sugar really *can* get kids to sit still and behave." Hornsby laughed. "But then I always wind up running out and winding up right back in the same place. Say, what was their reaction earlier when I told them to get to work? Do you think I was firm enough?" The girl suddenly looked confused. "Oh, you didn't hear me?" She shook her head. Hornsby laughed. "Then clearly, I wasn't firm enough." He paused. "What exactly did you see me doing?"

"Just sitting at your desk."

"You didn't hear me say anything?"

"No."

"Boy, I really need to speak up then. Thanks for the feedback. Say, what did it look like I was doing at my desk?"

"Reading some book."

This book again.

"Did you see if any kids came up with questions? What I'm trying to ask is, you know what can happen at times when you get lost in a book? Again, I'm just trying to get better as a teacher and can use expert feedback from a top student like yourself."

The girl turned and looked at the class. "Not this group. This group doesn't care enough to ask any questions." She pointed. "When any kid needs to use the bathroom, they just go over to the bin and grab a pass."

"Okay, thanks for the feedback. And what's your name again?"

"Angelina."

"Thank you, Angelina. You were a very big help."

Angelina headed back to her seat. "Oh, and Mr. Hornsby?"

"Yes, Angelina?"

"Someone came by and taped something to the door. But you didn't seem to notice."

Hornsby looked behind the door. His heart froze. *The Loyalists know about you.* "You didn't see who it was?"

"No."

Hornsby ripped it off the door. He called out, "Did anyone see who taped this to the door?" But all the kids appeared off in space. He walked around the hall, looking at the other doors in the hallway, but none of them had the same flyer taped to them. He poked his head into a couple of classrooms to ask the teachers. None of them knew anything about it.

He walked over to the hallway closet to check his phone. Maybe he should text Rosie to see if she saw anything. "Oh no."

Hornsby felt like he was going to throw up.

There were text messages written by him to Mr. Slattery.

The first one read, "If Waters was any older, he would be a mummified pharaoh."

The next one read, "Can you believe Waters wasn't drinking warm milk?"

He continued to scroll down through the horror script. "I'm shocked Waters was able to stand. He's so old."

"Did you see Water's false teeth almost fall out?"

But what was even more alarming than the text messages was how Slattery responded. First, he wrote, "That's terrible for you to joke about his age." Then he wrote, "Stop these mean text messages, Hornsby, you sound like a bully." Then he added, "Please don't text me anymore. I love Mr. Waters and do not want to read any more of your cruel attempts at humor. Please delete these immediately!"

This had Slattery's dirty hands written all over it.

In fact, Hornsby was grossed out just thinking about Slattery's actual filthy hands holding and touching his phone. He quickly moved his phone up and down his pant leg to try to wipe away the germs. But unfortunately, there was no way to delete the evidence.

Old Man Waters was the lone ally he had in his corner. That is until Slattery shows him the texts.

The bell rang. With the flyer about the Loyalists in one hand and his phone with the mean text messages in his other, Hornsby found his way to the bathroom in a total stupor.

"Why, hello there, Ethan…"

Of course. And who else besides Old Man Waters himself would just happen to be standing at the sink?

*****

It was like when you touch something hot and your body immediately repels on instinct. That was Hornsby's reaction once he saw the superintendent standing there, as he spun to exit. "How's your day going?" Too late.

Waters seemed to be acting totally normal, so Hornsby suspected Slattery hadn't gotten to him yet. He tried to calm himself down to not appear so unhinged. "My day is good. Yourself, Mr. Waters?"

Waters offered a big smile. "Haven't worked a day in my life."

Hornsby thought about what Rosie said about the odds of a very busy superintendent spending any more of his precious time observing subs was pretty slim, but this was his biggest fear. Just because Waters wasn't going to be entering his classroom didn't mean the threat was gone. There were millions of other reasons for a super-

intendent to be inside a school throughout the week. "Mr. Waters…
so…what brings you back into the building?"

"I'm here to watch the *We Love Literature* seminar being pre-
sented by the English department. You should make it your business
to pop your head in. We have plans for both English and social studies teachers to collaborate in the future on reading selections."

"Oh sure, that sounds like a wonderful opportunity. Do you
plan on staying around after the assembly?"

Waters appeared puzzled by the question. "Why?"

Hornsby tried to think of something quickly. "I thought to
maybe invite you back into my classroom…" *Oh my god! Why did
I just say that?* "You see I was going to be doing this exciting lesson
about the Civil War once I'm back covering for another social studies
teacher…" *Why am I saying this? Shut up, shut up, shut up…*

"Oh, okay. Sure. I would like to think of myself as somewhat of
a Civil War buff. Sounds like I would enjoy it. How about I look over
my schedule? We can find a time that works for both of us, all right?"

"No…not all right…"

"It's not?"

"No, it is…what I mean is… don't find a time… I mean…don't
worry about it… I don't want you to actually come in…" *Did I just
say that out loud?*

"You don't? But I thought you just invited me in?"

"I did… I mean… I do want that…but I…"

"Word of advice, Ethan?"

"Please."

"Relax a bit, okay? You can't teach to your potential when you're
constantly this nervous."

Hornsby took a deep breath and showed Waters his large exhale.
"Okay, Mr. Waters. Thank you for understanding. I know I can come
off as being too uptight. I really don't mean to be this way."

"I know what it's like to always feel you have to be proving
yourself. At my age, there are many doubters out there questioning
if I still got it."

Oh my god! Those text messages about his age!

Hornsby couldn't help but look at the age spots on his head and the small Band-Aid from the surgery. "What do you do about the doubters?"

"What I've always done. I do my job the best that I can because it's all I can control. Let me reassure you, Ethan, I'm impressed by your potential as a history teacher." He paused, and Hornsby could tell he was now referring to Peacock and Slattery. "And *my* opinion is still the one that matters most."

"Thank you, sir."

It was like a punch to the gut, the thought of Waters reading those mean text messages. Hornsby thought maybe he should say something to give him a heads up about what was coming, to just tell the truth, to use them as a showcase for how much of a bully Mr. Slattery is and what corrupt lengths he would go to. "Um, Mr. Waters…"

"Yes?"

But he also knew that when you're dealing with a real shyster like Slattery, who was dynamic enough to talk his way out of anything and had more fight in him than a heavyweight, just having the truth on your side was never going to be enough.

And the first rule as a new teacher was to stay as far under the radar as possible. The thought of bringing such childish behavior up to Waters and having to sit alongside Slattery in a finger-pointing he-said-he-said, as if they were still middle-school students about to be scolded, would surely leave a black mark on *both* of their records. Clearly, Slattery has realized this, which could only mean he has a much larger, more conniving plan in play. "Oh, don't worry about it, sir," said Hornsby.

Old Man Waters reached over for paper towels to dry his hands. "I wanted to ask you, Ethan, if you'd be willing to help out this weekend at the Relay for Life event up on the field. Cathy Baker is running it again this year, and she's always seeking volunteers. It's another great opportunity to pad your résumé."

Hornsby knew Relay for Life was a great cause, a top school fundraiser for cancer. "Absolutely, Mr. Waters. I'd be honored to help out. Should I reach out to Mrs. Baker?"

"Yes, please."

Hornsby continued to feel awful about the text messages, but it wasn't just about saving his own behind at this point. He mostly felt terrible at the thought of such an important, well-respected man, who he always admired, having his feelings hurt. Mr. Waters could have easily ridden off into the sunset years ago, but he stuck around because he cared. "You can count on me, sir."

Waters placed his gentle hand on Ethan's shoulder. "I'm glad you chose this school to come back to, Ethan. I love it when alumni are as passionate about our community as I am."

"Thank you, Mr. Waters."

13

"I agree with you, Ethan. Preston Slattery is up to something much bigger than just text messages," said Rosie. "Do you remember when little Stevie Backstrom used to take boxes of candy from his dad's shop and sell them to us?"

Hornsby put his hand on his belly. "I was probably his best customer. Ten cents per box of Red Hots, ten cents for each box of Alexander the Grape. And I would have paid anything for Lemonheads."

"Well, Mrs. Finkelstein warned him over and over to cut it out."

"But I saw Stevie still doing deals on the field during recess."

"So did Slattery and I. We both witnessed a multigrade gummy worm deal go down."

Hornsby began to understand why Rosie brought up little Stevie Backstrom. "But Slattery never went to Finkelstein about it. Because he got way more joy holding the information over Stevie's head and probably used it to get whatever he wanted the rest of the year."

"Yep. So not only do I think he intends to use the text messages to extort you all year, but I also think you have every right to worry that this is only phase one in a bigger plan to ruin you." Rosie paused. "Don't you think it's time you stuck up for yourself?"

"How? Punch him in the mouth? Beat him at his petty games? I would like to think I'm capable of acting like an adult."

"But you also can't keep letting him bully you."

Beep-beep…beep-beep…beep-beep… Rosie and Hornsby were startled by the blasting sounds of a fire drill coming from the speakers. Hornsby's nerves were already so tight. It felt like each of the sounds plucked on them like he was a cello. They followed the crowds of students out to the field. "Might as well spend my lunch period out here. I haven't had much of an appetite anyway."

There was Peacock, staring them down as they passed.

"It can't be good for your future being seen next to me," Hornsby said.

"She doesn't scare me."

But even with Old Man Waters reassuring him that he liked his potential, it didn't make Hornsby any less insecure when he was near Peacock. It felt to him like Peacock was continuing to glare right through his soul.

Hornsby took the flyer about the Loyalists out of his pocket. "I returned to this on my door."

"Oh my god."

"Someone in this building knows." Hornsby and Rosie looked around at all the faculty spread out across the field with their students. "We need to be suspicious of everyone."

"Maybe we're being watched right now?"

"I need another KitKat."

They both watched as Peacock, walkie-talkie in hand, walked over to the security guards to give directions. "I wasn't sure what to make of it," Rosie said, "but she was in the library this morning asking if you had taken out books or done searches on the Lost Colony of Roanoke."

"But how would she know?"

"Know what?"

"That *I was* actually doing a search of that old colony. And guess what? It turns out there was a Jane Pierce at Roanoke."

"You mean the same Jane Pierce from the journal in your secret closet?"

"Yep."

"Why is Roanoke called a lost colony?"

"It was an English colony located off the coast of North Carolina in the 1500s, but the king didn't get what he hoped for. Instead, the entire settlement of colonists just vanished, over a hundred of them."

"Like *completely* vanished?"

"Without a trace."

"Sounds like a mystery."

"It's one of America's great whodunits."

"But why is Peacock suddenly asking about it?"

Hornsby put his hands up. "If you're coming to me for answers about any of this, plan on failing the test."

"Well, don't worry, I would never tell her anything."

"I know you wouldn't." Hornsby faced Rosie. "You've always been a loyal friend."

"You too, Ethan."

"By the way, you should have seen Ben's mother. If you thought the parents at Upper Kakapo were tough, you should get a load of her."

"What did she do?"

"She pretty much thinks I was sent by the devil. And she's going to get in the way of what Ben really needs to grow."

"Then you need to fight for him."

"I tried to emphasize to him the importance of respecting his parent's rules and wishes. But it all backfired, and he became even more defiant toward his mother."

"What's Ben advocating for?"

"He only wants to help and play with his African American friend, Jeremiah."

"Then great. Good for him that he spoke up. He should do that."

"I know, but it's 1844, Rosie. Life was different. At this point, slavery still existed in the South, and there was racial prejudice even in the North. There was even a debate about what to do with new states when they are added, make 'em free or slave. Ben will become a civil rights leader. He will even follow his love of nature and sign into law, the Forest Reserve Act of 1891, setting aside forests for conservation. But I left behind a crying kid."

Rosie did a quick search on her phone. "Oh no."

Hornsby looked at the screen. He put his hands on his head. "Oh great, now Benjamin Harrison never becomes president either."

"What should we do?"

"I have to go back and fix both Calvin's and Ben's futures. Except I was the one to change them in the first place. Because I still have no idea why I'm being sent to these places and what I'm supposed to do when I get there." Hornsby sighed as he thought of his mother. "Oh, and to top it all off," he added, "I asked one of the girls in my class about what happens when I'm gone, and she also said there's a fake me sitting at my desk, reading a book."

"Then I definitely think it's time for us to go and see which book and why. And by us, I mean me."

"I agree."

The fire drill was ending. Security began to wave students and faculty back into the building. "That there's a fake you? It feels so creepy," said Rosie.

"If you want creepy, you should meet Mrs. Harrison." Hornsby looked at Rosie. "Wait a minute," he said to himself. "That might be exactly what I need you to do."

"I've been waiting for you to ask."

"But wait. I still don't know anything about these Loyalists, and what happens if we get separated? What if you can't get back?"

"When we were in Calvin's classroom, I didn't need to hold your hand to go back. So if we do get separated, just trust that I safely found my way back through the portal."

"Okay."

"When do we go?"

Hornsby put his hands up. "Now, I guess?"

14

Hornsby was peeking around, looking for Ben, while Rosie circled the Harrison den in awe. "Wow, look at this place. I feel like any second a tour guide is going to walk in." Instead, it was Charlotte. "Ah, Charlotte, may I introduce you to my partner, Ms. Mizrack."

Charlotte appeared bewildered by Rosie's presence. This strange-looking woman wore pants and a sweater, which no decent gal would ever be seen wearing in public. And she had all this jewelry and gold. Charlotte had served quite a few wealthy ladies through the years but had never seen a woman with more than one gold necklace on at a time. "Can you tell me where Benjamin is?"

Charlotte and Rosie were continuing to analyze each other's clothing. "He's by the barn."

"Thank you, Charlotte." Hornsby leaned in closer, whispering, "I'm so sorry for what I've caused. I promise to fix it and then stay out of your business forever."

Hornsby led Rosie to the porch. Her hair was blowing to the side as they were hit with blasts of cold wind. Trees were swaying across the landscape, and they could hear the animals nearby, growing edgy. Hornsby looked up at the sky, which was quickly transforming into a dark gray. "I can't believe I'm looking out onto the grounds of 1844. This feels so surreal," Rosie said.

Hornsby stepped in front to block her view. "Get focused. The Loyalists are out there, and I only need you to distract Mrs. Harrison for a few minutes so I can speak with Ben. Just promise, you'll cross back as soon as you can."

Rosie placed her hand to her forehead in salute. "Aye, aye, captain."

"Oh no, I forgot to bring the star stickers."

"You're giving out stickers?"

"I promised Ben. I gotta go back."

But it was too late.

"It's you that brings this uneasiness, Mr. Hornsby." It was Mrs. Harrison, who walked out onto the porch as the angry winds picked up. She saw Rosie. "And who is this?"

Hornsby was just about to introduce Rosie a second time as his assistant, Ms. Mizrack, until Rosie beat him to it. "I'm Mrs. Hornsby."

You are?

"My, um"—Rosie looked at Hornsby before looking back at Mrs. Harrison—"my husband asked if I could come to speak with you. Would that be okay, Mrs. Harrison?"

Mrs. Harrison also noticed the pants Rosie wore and all the gold around her neck and wrists. Then she examined Rosie's auburn high-lighted, wavy bobbed haircut, earrings, and all the pretty makeup on her face. "I didn't hear a carriage arrive?"

"We were, uh"—Rosie looked at Hornsby—"dropped off at the edge of the property."

"Dropped off?"

"Yes. Please, Mrs. Harrison. I came all this way to talk."

"All right, I have tea up. Please join me in the kitchen."

"Thank you."

Rosie looked back at Hornsby, who was in total shock. He mouthed, "Mrs. Hornsby?"

She whispered, "Go. I just bought you the time you need to fix history."

"You're sure you're ready for her?"

Rosie looked over as Mrs. Harrison was walking into the kitchen. "Oh, I think I can talk some sense into her."

Hornsby made a "you have no idea what you're in for" face.

*****

Rosie entered the tight kitchen, which had a cast-iron cooking stove against its far wall. It was hard to miss the residue stains from burnt wood all around it. On the adjacent wall, there was a wide-mouthed sink with what appeared to be a hand-operated pump for water. Across from it sat a small box that Rosie guessed might be an early version of the icebox. "What a lovely home you have, Mrs. Harrison."

Mrs. Harrison nodded. "I see from your jewels that you also come from a well-to-do home."

"We are lucky women to have had the fathers and now husbands to take such good care of us."

"Where is it you are from?"

"Ethan is a"—Rosie couldn't think of any better way to say it—"a traveling teacher. It affords us the chance to see the country. Good and bad."

Mrs. Harrison brought over the pot of tea and poured Rosie a full cup. "Yes, he mentioned that. You have no children?"

Rosie held her belly. "Only when God is ready to grant one. Mr. Hornsby." Rosie laughed. "He hopes for dozens."

Mrs. Harrison smiled. "Well, they always do, don't they? They aren't the ones having to nurse them."

"A woman's job in the home is so important. Your son is lucky to have you, Mrs. Harrison."

Finally, Rosie could tell Mrs. Harrison's concrete facade was beginning to crack. "Elizabeth. Call me Elizabeth."

"Well then…call me Rose."

"Rose. A beautiful name. I was very close to giving my first daughter, Mary, that name. May I ask about your hairstyle? I haven't seen such a short style before."

"My mother complains. She keeps telling me I'm too much on the cutting edge."

"What is the cutting edge?"

"What she means is that I'm up to date with the styles. They're wearing it this way in the big cities. When Ethan and I were in New York City, I just fell in love with it. But Mother, she's always complaining that I should grow it longer."

"And your mother is from which family?"

"The, uh…the Mizracks. My mother was a Mizrack."

"I haven't heard of that family."

"My grandfather comes from oil wealth."

"Oil wealth? Do you mean whale oils?"

"Oh, yes, he made fortunes in whale oils."

"He must have been brave."

"He sure was." Rosie could tell now was her best chance. "Mrs. Harrison… Elizabeth…my husband, he really means well. He just wants to help your boy."

"But that was never my concern."

"He told me all about your conversation. It's just that he believes, since Benjamin's great-grandfather was a signer of the Declaration of Independence and his grandfather was president, that Benjamin is also going to one day run for office."

"My son already knows that's what we're expecting."

"And one day, let's just hypothetically say, he does, oh I don't know, first become a senator and then become president, well, what's going to be asked of him?"

"Only the Lord will know."

"But we can assume by then more states will have been added to the country."

"We can."

"And that if there is a war with the South and blacks are freed for good, they will need strong voices to speak up for them."

"Mr. Hornsby and I already agreed a war with the South would happen at some point."

Rosie added, "And as we move our wagons west, someone is going to also have to speak up about our need to preserve our natural forests for future generations."

Mrs. Harrison seemed intrigued. "And you think the voice of the Lord will enter Benjamin's mind?"

"Oh, yeah. Big voice of the Lord." Rosie held her hands out wide. "Real big."

Mrs. Harrison was thinking it through. "And your husband believes my son will be able to attain such great feats if he is allowed to play with Jeremiah?"

"He believes it can have a positive influence."

"Your husband's intentions belong to the Lord?"

Rosie nodded. But suddenly, it felt to Rosie as if the room was growing colder as Mrs. Harrison's temperament reversed back. "You think I'm some foolish woman, do you?"

"No...no... I just thought...a couple of fine Christian ladies sitting down to talk. We can always solve what our men can't..."

"You think because you walked into a small farmhouse with that city hair and all that gold around your neck that my husband and family aren't also powerful?"

"No, no. I know who your family is. Believe me, I know..."

"Nothing gets solved. Except I want both you and your gypsy husband to leave my home immediately. And I don't want you anywhere near my son, Benjamin."

*****

Hornsby found Ben in front of the barn, brushing down Chestnut. It looked like the trees down the hill were about to snap in half from the relentless wind. "Mr. Hornsby!"

"Hi, Ben."

Ben ran up to Hornsby with a hug. "I couldn't wait. Did you bring my star stickers?"

"I'm so sorry, Ben, but I didn't."

"But you crossed your heart. You promised me. And I was a good listener."

Hornsby was dying inside. He could still hear Ben's cries, and he felt responsible for what happened. But he realized, forgetting the star stickers could actually work to his advantage. Every new teacher dreamed of having learning moments with students, and now Hornsby knew this was his. "I know what I promised, but the deal was only the best listeners get stickers."

"But I was."

"Let's take this time to reflect. In what ways did you not listen?"

"I reckon because of my ma?"

"Yes, Ben. You need to be more respectful of her rules. I *stressed* that to you."

"But I want to be half pa, half grandpa, like you said I should."

"And you will be when the time is right. You're a fine young man, and I'm really proud of who you are."

Just then Charlotte and Jeremiah walked from the small cottage toward the barn. The wind was continuing its assault. She instructed Jeremiah to get the team of horses into the barn, but Ben didn't hesitate to rush over and help. Both boys walked them in and tied them up. But Ben made sure to walk right back out to Hornsby. "Was that okay, Mr. Hornsby?"

Hornsby smiled. "You're a gentleman, Ben. Now how 'bout a game of soldiers and Indians?"

"Really?"

"Just no real rifles or arrows this time." Hornsby laughed.

Hornsby looked over at the old barn. The entire structure was rattling. He was wondering why Jeremiah was still in there with restless horses and an approaching storm. "I'm gonna get you, you Indian!" Ben was already in chase mode. Hornsby took off down the hill and jumped the stream, but Ben was immediately on his tail. Hornsby faked getting shot and rolled around the grass for extra effect. "Now I'm the Indian!" Ben yelled. He took off toward the woods. But Hornsby didn't follow. Instead, he was stuck, still wondering when Jeremiah would appear from the barn. He inched closer to look inside.

The entire moment hit Hornsby like a ton of bricks. It was when he realized Trigger had kicked the broken wagon off its stilts right onto Jeremiah. He lay there, lifeless.

Hornsby no longer felt as if he was back in time. Instead, he felt frozen in it.

The screams he did now hear were Ben's, who came up from behind. They lifted the wagon off Jeremiah. Hornsby ran out to see if Charlotte or Mrs. Harrison could call for help, but then remembered, there was no 911 to dial in 1844.

Mrs. Harrison was already standing about twenty-five yards away, dress blowing, shotgun in hand. "This is an evil you brought." She aimed her shotgun right at him and fired. Hornsby hit the ground, scared out of his mind, as he watched her open the barrel to place another bullet inside. He only had a few seconds to get himself into the farmhouse. He ran with all his might to the front door. Another bullet just missed him putting a hole in it.

All of a sudden, Chestnut came flying out of the barn. It was Ben riding her with Jeremiah lying on his lap.

They were headed toward the road.

15

"I'm done. I'm outta here," a frustrated Hornsby said to Rosie as he rushed down the hallway and headed for the side doors of Upper Kakapo.

Yet Rosie wore a monster smile as she spoke a million miles an hour. "I still can't believe it! There was this really awesome-looking stove! I felt like I was in a movie! And her dress! I couldn't take my eyes off it! I could see the uneven hand stitching! The tea tasted like such garbage, though. I was just so tempted to ask if it was a new flavor from Starbucks, just to see her reaction!"

"Glad you're having so much fun with this," Hornsby snapped, "but Jeremiah could be dead."

"What?"

"And Ben took off on a horse he can't handle in the middle of a storm and probably got Wizard of Oz-ed somewhere miles away."

"Oh my god. So you just left?"

"Yeah, I just left. The next thing I knew, the old witch was shooting at me. She practically took the entire inside of her house out. I had to crawl through the den on all fours just to make it back to our hallway."

"Oh my god."

"Yeah, oh my god. Real bullets, Rosie. *Real!*" Hornsby rubbed his forehead. "But you know what? Who cares? Calvin Coolidge, Benjamin Harrison, a couple of nobody presidents. No one ever talks about them, anyway, so no one would ever notice, right? So what the Great Depression lasted practically a decade longer than it was supposed to and more people suffered because Coolidge was never president? So what about Harrison pleading for civil rights in this country? The South wasn't listening anyway, right? And who really cares about the conservation movement or national parks? Teddy Roosevelt came along after to finish that job, so who needs Harrison anyway? Goodbye, Rosie. Goodbye, Upper Kakapo. I quit!" Hornsby stormed through the doors.

"Wait, Ethan, don't leave. Please." Hornsby stopped. "Maybe if you put in for a transfer to another building, time traveling would stop. Maybe if you went to another district, it stops. But please don't throw away a chance at a career you've dreamed of."

Hornsby felt so dejected. In a somber voice, he added, "I'm not throwing it away. Uncontrollable time traveling is."

Rosie did a quick search on her phone. "Look! You did it!"

Hornsby looked at the screen. "Ben is back to being the twenty-third president?"

"He is! See, you can do it, Ethan. Now you just need to figure out how to get back to Calvin."

"But how?"

"I don't know. But I did get a real good look at the book. It's made of brown leather. Someone ripped out a bunch of pages in the back, and it's bound by string."

"What book?"

"The one you were reading."

"Who was reading?"

"Fake you. By the way, you're very nice."

"Wait. You actually talked to fake me?"

"Yeah, and I think I like him better," Rosie joked.

"Fake me really talks?"

"Fake you not only talks. He really is just like an authentic clone of you. Minus the KitKat wrapper that's usually hanging out of your pocket."

Hornsby needed a seat. Since there was none, he instead walked back inside and leaned against the wall. "You said bound by a string?"

"Uh, huh."

"That means fake me was reading the Jane Pierce journal."

"But how could he be? You said Mr. Wells has it?"

"I don't know." Hornsby thought it over. "How has any of this been possible?"

"Maybe there are more clues in that secret closet of yours?"

"Well, it was real dark last night, and I only had the light from my phone…" Hornsby checked the time. He had an idea. "Can you follow me back to my house at the end of the day?"

"I'll meet you in the parking lot after the last bell."

"Great. I think it's time we get to the bottom of why that stuff was hidden in my house."

*****

"You don't have too many people over, do you, Ethan?" Rosie inferred as she observed the complete mess that was Hornsby's house. "Do you not even have a TV?"

"I prefer to just read."

Rosie looked around some more, noticing books everywhere. "That's for sure."

"Do you need to use the bathroom?"

She peeked in. "No… I'm good." But then she threw on her classic Rosie smile. "It's all really nice, Ethan."

"Thanks."

She wandered over to the small table in the living room. "Is this your mother?" Hornsby nodded. "How old were you here?"

"Eight or nine, I think."

"How did she die?"

"She didn't. Well, maybe she's dead now. But at the time, she just left."

"I'm so sorry, Ethan. I had no idea. How old were you?"

"Seventh grade. I remember the detectives searched and searched for her. Truthfully, I'm not sure if I should hope she's dead or not." Hornsby began to choke up. "To think that maybe she is alive somewhere but doesn't care enough to call me…"

Rosie reached out and held Hornsby's hand. "I'm so, so sorry for you, Ethan."

84

"It was really hard. Maybe that's why I want so badly to work at our school. I still remember how much the teachers were there for me when I returned."

"What about your dad?"

"Never knew him. Passed away before I was born. But the thing about my family is my mom always told me I also had aunts and uncles and grandparents, but I never met any of them either."

"But you have pictures, right?"

"I have nothing of any of them."

Rosie was puzzled. "How could a family have zero pictures of each other?"

"Welcome to the Hornsbys, the strangest family on Earth. It's what it is, I guess. I did register for one of those genetic family origins things. I sent in my DNA, and all that came back was that both my parents are from England." He pushed aside broken drywall pieces. "Here's the secret closet."

Rosie peeked in noticing the mouse skeleton. "Oh my god, I'm gonna throw up."

Hornsby rushed into the kitchen to grab a towel and garbage bag. "Sorry, I'm sure you can tell, I haven't had the chance to clean up yet." He dropped the mouse into the garbage bag. "If only he could talk, maybe he would have our answers."

Rosie entered carefully and began to inspect the small closet. She ran her hand along the shelf. She then circled the room and knocked on the walls. "Think there's another room hidden behind this one?"

"Nope. That's my bedroom. And that side leads to the kitchen."

"What if there's a hidden staircase below?"

"Nope, just slab under this tile."

"What about up there?"

"I was recently up there. Just attic."

"Then I guess there aren't any more clues here."

Hornsby slid his body down the wall and sat. "I guess it's a dead end." Rosie sat down next to him. It was quiet. Hornsby continued to wish the dead mouse could speak. "Wait a minute, the mouse had to get in here somehow, right?"

"Yes. There must be a mousehole around here, somewhere."

Hornsby began to examine the walls for any small openings, checking every inch. Then he looked up. "Wait here."

Rosie remained in the secret closet, listening to Hornsby's footsteps as he made his way up the attic ladder and across the attic floor. Rosie heard his voice through a tiny hole in the ceiling. "Looks like our friend does want to talk."

"What did you find?"

"Right above this hole, he left us a prize. I've got the chewed piece of canvas."

Rosie waited for Hornsby in the kitchen. "And it fits like a perfect puzzle piece."

"Maybe it's the Mona Lisa?" Rosie laughed.

Hornsby laughed as well. "I doubt I just became really rich overnight."

"Do you think it's our Jane Pierce?"

Hornsby was looking at it from every angle, tilting his head, stepping in close, and even stepping back. Then he squinted his eyes just to be sure. "No. It's definitely not Jane Pierce."

*****

"That's my mom," said Hornsby, placing the painting on the counter in front of Mr. Wells.

"Can you at least introduce me to your friend?"

"I'm sorry, Mr. Wells, this is my friend Rosie."

"Nice to meet you, Rosie."

"Nice to meet you as well, Mr. Wells."

"Look, it's her." Hornsby pointed. "Look at her eyes, the nose."

"But it's hand-painted, Ethan."

"By obviously a really good artist. I know it's her."

"We might have ourselves Jane Pierce. But I think it's a stretch to say it's your mom."

Hornsby pointed again. "Look at her chin. I just know it's her."

"Slow down, Ethan. We're talking about a hand-painted piece with a tear, and it doesn't make sense that your mom would be the subject."

"I'm not gonna slow down. Please. I also know it was her hand-writing in the journal."

"I think you *want* to believe that."

"I *do* believe that." Mr. Wells was quiet. "And if you can't help me, I'll go to another antique dealer. I'll even bring a police forensic team into my home to examine and fingerprint. And I'm not gonna stop until I get to the bottom of this."

Wells appeared alarmed by the threat. He finally nodded his head in forfeit. "Okay, you two, wait for me in the back room. Let me grab the journal."

Hornsby and Rosie waited by what appeared to be an antique card table. "Please don't be afraid to sit at her. It's better built than anything today."

"Is everything in here an antique?" asked Rosie.

"If not, close enough." Wells took a seat. He had the Pierce journal in his hand. "I knew this day would come, and I'm sorry, Ethan, for holding back on you." Wells still appeared hesitant but then thought it over once more. "Eh, what's the difference at this point? Even if you go and scream about what I'm going to tell you, no one would believe you anyway." He opened the journal. "The truth is your mother was not supposed to keep the evidence. We swore we would eliminate all remnants of our past."

"But how could this possibly be her past?"

"I'm just warning you, Ethan. You're not ready for what I have to tell you. There was a good reason why I've kept you in the dark."

"My father's dead, and my mother abandoned me, Mr. Wells. There's nothing else that can hurt me."

Wells cleared his throat. "The artifacts you brought to me do indeed date back to the 1580s. And yet the reason they do not appear as old as they should is that they're not actually four hundred-plus years old. Your mother and all her possessions actually traveled through time." Hornsby and Rosie looked at each other. "As did I, along with her."

"What?"

"I told you, you wouldn't be ready for this."

"I don't understand, Mr. Wells."

"How could you? But the truth is that centuries ago, your mom and I, along with over a hundred others, set sail from England to establish the colony of Roanoke."

Rosie said, "We learned that colony was lost."

"Oh, sure, it was lost all right. That's because here we are." Hornsby's and Rosie's minds were blown. Wells said, "Our task was to settle a colony for the Crown. But we were unprepared for what was in front of us. The conditions, they became impossible for survival. We lived through a starving period. For months, we had very little to eat. That's when we lost your father, Ethan. He gave every last berry to your pregnant mother. Others, they died of fever, some infection. By the time our first brutal winter was over, we didn't have enough clothes, food, or medicines to even consider trying to survive another year. Your mother, she wanted to go back to England."

"Why didn't you?"

"We had stubborn leaders, truly, truly stubborn. We befriended an Algonquian tribe who taught us how to grow food for a spring harvest, how to hunt, but we were desperate. And our leaders made the grand mistake of betraying them. There was greed in the colony, and our leaders believed we should only be growing tobacco for England. They also felt natives should be murdered if they didn't serve us or our Lord. But these Algonquins were believers in the spirits of nature, that there were powers beyond anything we could understand from our god, that special forces run our natural world, and that if you betray nature, dimensions will overlap."

"Was your colony still able to make peace with them?"

"No. And their chief put a curse on us. He asked the spirits of nature to send our entire colony, along with all our possessions, off into a world so far away from them that we could never hurt them again. Nature answered. But it was not in a way anyone expected. Instead of a far-off land, it was to a far-off year. Four hundred years into the future."

"Then that's why there are no family pictures, Ethan. They all were living in England in the 1500s," observed Rosie.

"What happened once you landed four hundred years into the future?"

"Imagine it, over a hundred of us in our raggedy clothes, filthy, very few possessions. We saw cars, modern homes, green grass, restaurants. It was unimaginable. You name it. We weren't ready for 1987. Oh, no."

"Where did you go?" asked Rosie.

"We did the only thing simple farm folk knew how to do, we went to church. There happened to be a savior from the Lord there in this local church, a priest who opened his doors for us." Wells laughed. "He got one good look at us and immediately locked the doors behind to others. He sat us down, listened to our tale, and said a prayer."

"He believed you?"

"I still doubt he ever did. Who could believe such a crazy tale? Fortunately for us, though, he saw it through the Lord's eyes and said we were children of God. He made it his responsibility to care for us. The church had just done a huge clothing drive, and we were able to get fitted for modern outfits. He fed us off volunteer donations, found us shelters. Later on, our group decided to change our names just in case this curse continued. I was now James Wells. Your mother was now Jane Hornsby."

"Did you go back to the church?"

"Oh, sure. Where else would we go for necessities? Each morning, he taught us what we would need. We read together. We did math. We even got a chance to see a TV for the first time and hear a radio. To tell you the truth, we all felt relieved we no longer had to starve through another vicious winter. There were heat and warm blankets. It began to dawn on us that this was no curse. Instead, it was a blessing. And you, Ethan Hornsby...the boy who was supposed to be the very first birth...the first English child to be born in history on American soil, was instead born in 1987, in a real hospital with real nurses. I never saw your mother as happy and relieved."

"I can't get my head around any of this," said Hornsby.

"Imagine if you got whisked into the year 2400, that was what it was like for us."

Rosie thought about Hornsby's sudden ability to travel back in time and asked, "What about going back to your era? Did you guys try it? Like, were you able to reverse the curse?"

Suddenly, Well's demeanor seemed to change. "I think you now have what you were looking for, Ethan. I think that's all I can say about it."

"Can you please excuse us for a second, Mr. Wells?" Hornsby grabbed Rosie's hand and led her into another room. "I gotta tell him."

"No. Absolutely not. Do you even believe his story?"

"I do. I mean, I want to. I mean, how else can my heritage be explained? His story is the only thing that makes sense. Plus, all of a sudden, I have this power to travel through time."

Rosie glanced over at Wells sitting at the card table. She whispered, "Look around this place. He's probably using his power to go back and collect antiques. Making fortunes."

"Well, then I need to learn how he's doing it. Because I haven't been able to bring any evidence back with me." Hornsby sighed. "Look, Rosie, I know this whole thing is nuts, and I understand this is not the time to trust what this man is telling us, but if it wasn't for him looking out for me, I would've been stuck in a foster home without even pencils for school."

"I don't know, Ethan. I'm just not getting a good vibe from him."

"Please, Rosie."

"Okay."

They sat back down at the card table. "Please just let me know if my mom was able to travel back in time?"

It was an emphatic "No. The only thing your mother did was give it her all in this new world. She got cleaned up, learned about modern menus, money, and took a job as a waitress in a local diner. Before long, she was a manager. And she was taking wonderful care of you."

"Was my mother the only woman in the colony?"

Wells suddenly tightened up again. If this was a card game, at this old table, both Hornsby and Rosie could tell that Wells wasn't ready to show his hand.

But Rosie was done tiptoeing around. "I'll take it that means there were other women."

"Take it however you would like."

"We can always do a Google search to find out who else was on that ship."

"Do whatever makes you happy."

"And what about you, Mr. Wells," Rosie continued, "are you a time traveler?"

Wells checked his watch. "I think we're done here."

"I'll take that also as a yes."

Wells leaned in closer, annoyed to the brim by Rosie's arrogance. "You have no idea what you're asking about. And you're not in any way prepared for the answers you think you want."

Hornsby caught Rosie's facial expression as she was trying to use her eyes to tell him not to spill the beans. "Please, Mr. Wells, we're not trying to be any type of threat to you or to try to ruffle any feathers here. I really do just need answers. Because I can time travel. And I have no idea how to control any of it."

Wells leaned back, placing his hand on his chin. "Well, that explains it. The one person from our colony who didn't keep her time-traveling powers was your mother. None of us could explain it. Why her? But now I know the answer. She passed the power along through her womb."

"It just started to happen. Every time I enter a classroom."

"Then that's how it will always happen."

"Why?"

There was a jingle at the front door. "I'm sorry, you two, but I've got a customer." He stood in the doorway. "I hope I've helped."

"But Mr. Wells?" Hornsby pleaded. "I... I just get sent to places. I don't know why or how or what to do when I get there."

"Your natural instincts are your best friend. Remember, this curse was created by natural spirits, and it continues to be guided by them. There's a certain harmony to the natural process, and when it's interrupted, you can almost hear it." Hornsby thought of when he heard the female voice. "If you don't have a proper balance in your life, it's going to feel as if traveling is controlling you. Not vice versa."

"And what if I need to stay back in time for an extended period?"

"Time marches at the same speed. If you spent a day over there, a day over here also goes by. I guess my advice for a traveling teacher would be to plan on traveling on a Friday. It'll buy the weekend."

Hornsby and Rosie looked at each other. Tomorrow was Friday. *Oh no, I promised Mrs. Baker and Old Man Waters I would be available this weekend to help at the Relay for Life event.*

"But what about this fake me, this twin, who stays here in my absence?" But Wells was already down the hallway.

"You okay, Ethan?" asked Rosie.

"Why was my fake me reading this journal? And how can I control him so that I can keep a regular existence?"

"Mr. Wells said there was a certain harmony to the natural process. That you're being sent back in time as a teacher to children who need your help and that your fake self was reading your mother's journal. It does make some sense. It's who you are."

"I can't have him just sitting at a desk."

"Maybe you should ask Mr. Wells about it the next chance you get."

"And how can I control my travels?"

Rosie shrugged her shoulders. "I guess take Mr. Well's advice and try to find a more natural balance in your life."

Wells popped his head back in. "I'm sorry again, but this customer is gonna be here a while."

"We're sorry, we will go, Mr. Wells."

"Before you do, try these on." It was a woman's hat and a gentleman's cap that looked like they were from the early 1900s. "Looks like perfect fits."

Rosie looked at Wells suspiciously. "But how did you know?"

"That you also traveled? It was obvious. Plus, this Ethan over here is a smart one. It obviously didn't take him long to figure out how to bring someone along."

"Look at us. I could be a suffragette."

"And I could be on my way to work at the original Detroit Ford factory."

*****

But it wasn't really a customer. It was Lou Boyd, the deep voice over the phone, who was also the oldest remaining colonist from Roanoke. He used his cane as support to sit his fragile body down alongside the display case. "He's not in control yet," said Wells.

"But I can feel it. His ability is strong," responded Lou. "It's unlike any source of power I've been around."

"Because he was born with it."

Lou straightened out the pleats of his pants. "I suspect the Loyalists are onto him."

"If we knew about him, then they certainly do," said Wells. He thought about Rosie. "And that friend of his, she could be a problem."

Lou didn't hesitate. "Then take care of it."

"Only when the time is right."

Lou's eyes zeroed in on Wells. "Time. It's all we have."

16

The next morning, Hornsby was waiting for Rosie in front of his classroom, but he received a very different visitor. "Milk and sugar." It was the swindler, Mr. Slattery.

"I don't even know what you're talking about."

"It's how I take my coffee. And don't forget, hot during the winter, iced come spring, and on my desk, first thing every day."

"Sounds like I'm getting off cheap. I thought you'd be extorting me for gourmet lunches."

"When dealing with a struggling learner like yourself, *Thorns*by…a quality teacher like myself knows to start you off slow, build up some confidence. But don't worry, the tasks will get more challenging. I hope you're going to be up for it. I'd hate to have to call home, considering there's no one there."

"You know, Slattery, all it would take for me to have you jailed is to have them pull the camera footage of you stealing my phone right out of my jacket pocket."

"You mean from this closet?" Slattery walked over to the hallway closet to show Hornsby that he also kept his coat inside it. "Don't you mean I was caught on video going into my *own* pocket for my *own* phone? Of course, I'd never be stupid enough to leave my phone in my jacket pocket."

"I know you're too smart to show the text messages to Waters. You and I both know how it could backfire on you."

"Who said anything about showing it to Old Man Waters? Oh, and check out this little beauty." Slattery showed Hornsby a picture on his phone of Hornsby sitting at his desk, reading, while class was going on. "Catch ya' later, *Thorns*by." As he headed down the hallway, he added, "A little extra sugar in my coffee on Mondays. You know, it being Monday and all."

Rosie finally made it. "What took you so long?" Hornsby asked.

"With everything going on, I totally forgot about this librarian meeting we were scheduled for this morning. Next thing I know, two librarians from the high school are waiting for me."

"Oh, no. Is everything okay?"

Rosie entered the room first. "Yeah, it's fine. But I totally get what you're feeling right now. Your face makes it look like you're listening to someone, but your mind is in a million other places."

"I spent the night trying to better understand how I can achieve some natural-balanced thing in my life and to find some sort of harmony with nature, but the truth is, I'm different than the others. The natives from that time lived off the land, so did the colonists. They were born connected to the stars, to their animals, to the Earth beneath their feet. Me? The closest way I connect to nature is by checking the weather app on my phone or searching for vacation destinations. I barely even like being outside." Hornsby sat down at the teacher's desk. "I guess I can try meditation or maybe give yoga a shot."

"Can you even sit Indian style?"

"Not without splitting my pants."

"Hold off on the meditation and yoga for now."

"By the way, there were eight other women besides my mom at Roanoke."

"And children did make the voyage. I did a little digging of my own."

Hornsby examined his new room. "I was asked to team with Ms. Bean today and Monday to assist her with her small group of students since Ms. Shaw is out sick."

Ms. Bean was also the teacher who helped Rosie in the library. "Perfect timing. As long as she's in the room, you won't have to travel at all today."

"Team-teaching. It may be one of my future remedies. It'll be nice to spend the day helping out *today's* kids."

Mrs. Baker, the math teacher who was running Relay for Life, popped in. "There you are, Ethan. Oh, hi there, Rosie."

"Hi."

"Ethan, I just wanted to make sure you got the instructions I left in your mailbox."

"Got 'em. And all ready to go."

"I can't say thank you enough. I really appreciate the help. Fingers crossed about the weather."

Hornby held up his crossed fingers as Mrs. Baker left.

"No, you didn't," said Rosie.

"Of course, I did. I ran into Old Man Waters in the bathroom. What was I supposed to say, no?"

"But what about what Wells said about needing to take advantage of the weekends?"

"That's exactly what I intend to do."

"How? You just locked yourself into being up on that field all day tomorrow."

"Just go home on your break, grab your old hat from Well's shop, throw on a dress that reaches your feet, and meet me back here by the end of the day."

Rosie smiled with exuberance. "You're gonna take me with you again?"

"If there's one thing I've learned for sure, it's that I can't do any of this without you."

Rosie smiled again. "What happens if we can't get back to Calvin?"

"We have to. I must figure out a way to rescue the Roaring Twenties. It's all I've been thinking about." Suddenly, Hornby's nerves struck as he thought about the threat from the Loyalists. His instincts began to tell him not to involve Rosie in the next trip.

"What's wrong, Ethan?"

"Oh, nothing. Let's just not get shot by Mrs. Harrison."

"Good idea." Rosie stopped at the door and turned. "Catch ya' later, *Thorns*by."

"Very cute."

*****

Hornsby held Rosie's hand, and they were suddenly transformed into another place and time. But it was not a classroom or a home. Instead, it was an entrance to a ballpark. Good thing they had their hats. Everyone else was wearing one, particularly all the gentlemen, most of whom also sported suits. They heard the crack of a bat, and the crowd erupted. Hornsby figured the time period must be sometime in the early 1900s, as the seats in the ballpark were all bleacher style. The place felt overly snug, and the large billboards were covered in advertisements for products with prices as low as five cents. "I guess all that thinking and wishing about getting back to Calvin's classroom didn't work," observed a disappointed Hornsby. "Clearly, I'm still not in control of my time travels. And how come this time, no one is waiting for me, like when Mr. Begget and Charlotte were expecting me as a teacher?"

"Maybe this trip will somehow connect to Calvin. Let's look around to see if we can find a connection."

Hornsby and Rosie got closer to the ball field, and he made out the uniforms. It was the Boston Red Sox versus Cleveland Indians. He checked around the dirty ground for a ticket stub. "May 25, 1919. Holy cow! We're in Fenway Park, in Boston." Hornsby took off his hat. "I need to sit down." Finding seats wasn't difficult. The park was two-thirds empty. He couldn't tell if his heart was sprinting from heavy nerves or sky-high excitement.

"I thought Fenway Park was that stadium with the giant green wall?" Rosie asked.

"They'll call that the Green Monster, but it's not built yet." Hornsby and Rosie could see homes and buildings from their seats.

"For a famous park, it feels like I'm sitting at a high school baseball game."

"This was how it was back then." Hornsby's heart hadn't slowed. "I can't believe this. The year 1919 was Babe Ruth's last year as a Red Sox player. Only a few months from now, he'll be sold to the Yankees, and the rest is history." Hornsby's eyes popped out of his head as he saw it was the Babe on the mound. "There he is!"

"I thought he hit home runs?"

Hornsby pointed. "You see how far out those fences are? By this point, it was so hard to hit home runs here that the Babe was mostly a pitcher for the Sox and a real good one. But in a few years, he'll be crushing homers for the Yankees and become the most popular person in the country." Hornsby thought it over. "But the Babe can't be the reason I'm here, right? So what is?"

"Come on, let's see what else is happening." Hornsby owed it to himself to take a few more minutes to watch the game. "Come on, Ethan, it's going to get dark soon."

The two began to walk the small ballpark looking for whatever clues they could find. Hornsby kept asking, "But why Boston?" He couldn't specifically recall if Calvin was supposed to become the governor of Massachusetts in 1919 until he altered history. Both Rosie and Hornsby swore to no longer take being able to look something up on their smartphones for granted.

"Excuse us." They were accidentally bumped by four gentlemen wearing top hats and bowties as they tried to head down steps to their seats in the front row. Hornsby heard, "Those are our seats right there, Senator."

Hornsby pulled Rosie aside. "He said 'Senator.' I have to go down there to see who it is. At first glance, I think it's Warren Harding."

"Who's that?"

"Of course," Hornsby said, "Harding's from Ohio. Maybe he's here to see his Cleveland Indians. But Warren Harding's the guy who'll be running for president next year in 1920 and win by a landslide. And guess who's supposed to be his vice president?"

"You're kidding? Calvin?"

"But somewhere along the way, it never happened. The Roaring Twenties can't happen without Harding first as president and then Coolidge second. They're the dynamic duo of smaller government and lower taxes. Calvin is the first VP to sit in on cabinet meetings, so he has a big say under the Harding administration. We *have* to make sure Calvin gets into office."

"Why did Harding only serve one term if he was so popular?"

Hornsby looked down at the men. "He's going to die three years into office."

Rosie noticed Harding began to munch away on a snack. "Should we warn him he needs to eat better?"

"Back in this day, men dropped dead all the time without warning. You went to bed each night with your fingers crossed that you'd wake up in the morning. Doctors weren't monitoring blood pressure, checking cholesterol levels or finding cancer early enough." Hornsby looked again. "I have to get down there to him."

"But what can you possibly do? It's not like he's going to listen to us anyway."

"I have to try." Hornsby thought about what he had read about Harding. "After he dies, America learns how corrupt some of his cabinet members were." Hornsby thought to himself, *Maybe there is a way to make him listen.* "If history tells us anything about that snack-eating senator down there, it's that his pals will listen to any bribe if the price is right." Rosie's wide-brimmed hat and long dress gave Hornsby an idea. "The year 1919 is also the year you ladies first get voting rights."

"Which means next year will be our first presidential election."

"Which means Warren Harding is going to care quite a bit about your support. Stand here so he can see you."

Hornsby made his way down the steps to the front row. The crowd erupted as Babe Ruth struck out another Indian. "Excuse me, um, Senator?"

But the man who turned to talk was a much slimmer and shorter gentleman. "Please allow the senator to enjoy the game."

Hornsby pointed up the stairs. "You see that young woman there? She's the new head of the NWSA, which you know is a woman's suffrage organization. And she's rather upset that Senator Harding has refused to take her calls regarding his upcoming campaign for president."

That got Harding to turn around. He whispered into Slim's ear, who asked, "How would she know that? The senator has yet to announce his intentions."

Hornsby made sure to say it loud enough for all to hear. "It seems as if you gentleman are the only ones to *not* know…that your secret is out."

Hornsby watched the four men huddle. He heard from behind, "Sit down! I can't see the game."

Slim said, "Senator Harding will be happy to speak with the NWSA. Please tell the nice lady to call again. He'll be back in Washington tomorrow and is looking forward to her call."

"Sit down!" Hornsby heard again as another man screamed from behind.

"This can't wait. The NWSA also needs to know right away if they'll have the senator's vote for ratification of the Nineteenth Amendment, which you know is only days away."

Slim replied, "Please remind her that the senator has always supported the amendment. Now anything else, please call or visit his office."

"We both know that's not true. He has *not* always supported women's suffrage."

Harding snarled as he spun his head back around at Hornsby. The four men rehuddled.

"Sit down!"

Hornsby felt a tight grip around his arm. It was a Boston cop wearing a uniform that featured a standard police cap with two strips of buttons down the front and a long leather belt across the chest and a holster with a gun and nightstick. Hornsby noticed two other items of note: his name was Officer Schneider, and he wasn't wearing standard leather boots. "Let's go."

"Please, Senator." Hornsby made one last attempt. "There's a large block of female votes either going to you or James Cox next year."

Harding turned to look at Rosie one more time, and Hornsby could see it all over his face. "How could these two possibly know who my democratic opponent is going to be?"

As Hornsby was being pushed up the steps, he added, "The Parker Hotel at seven o'clock, everything you want to know about your opponent."

As Hornsby was being escorted out of Fenway Park, he said to Rosie, "You couldn't warn me he was coming?"

"I was trying to get your attention."

Both got shoved out into the street.

*****

Timeworn Boston: cobblestone streets, packs of kids without parents, crowds all in their Sunday best even on a Friday evening, Brass era cars in the streets, most without roofs, all driven by men, honking horns that sounded as if they should belong to circus clowns, and there were no traffic lights. Hornsby and Rosie were careful to cross. It felt as if the roads had no rules because most likely, they didn't. And then there was the extraordinary number of food carts and stands. It seemed as if you could get anything to eat from freshly cut meat to just-picked fruits. "I could go for one of those juicy-looking plums," said Rosie.

To her surprise, Hornsby reached into his pocket and handed over a penny. "How do you have money from back in this time?"

"Lincoln has been on the penny since 1909," Hornsby whispered back. "Just pray he doesn't check the date."

Rosie slowly bit in to savor every bit of flavor. She looked around, inhaled the freshest air, gazed into Ethan's eyes, and wrapped her arm around his. "Look around, Ethan. Only the luckiest girl on Earth is experiencing this right now. Oh, we should go see what Boston Commons looks like. And Quincy Market must be a sight too. Do you think you have enough pennies to buy us dinner? We can sit in one of those cafés down there, and people watch. And then we can go shopping."

Hornsby felt it in his heart. He loved how happy Rosie was and knew that she was right. They should try to turn this into a night they would never forget. Yet he was rattled to his core. First, he was still wondering who the Loyalists were and if they were in Boston, and there were the packs of orphans. It seemed as if every little kid on the corner was sizing him up for an easy pickpocket. Then as they passed each building stoop, there seemed to be another Irishman making eye contact, as if a mob hit was coming—and the cops too. There were plenty of them, yet they projected the opposite of a feeling of security. There was nothing more dangerous than a man in uniform who was on the take.

And he couldn't stop thinking about Harding and Coolidge and how he only had a short time to fix history before needing to get back for the Relay for Life.

But there was Rosie's warmth and the aroma of her soft perfume, her gentle arm gripping his even tighter as the bright moon began to glisten, creating chills he had never felt before.

Here's what he wanted to say to Rosie, "I'm sorry, we're working, and we only have one hour before we need to be at the Parker Hotel to see if Harding and his companions show." Instead, here's what he did say, "Okay, we can go to Quincy Market."

Rosie made sure to take their several block stroll as slowly as possible, peeking into every storefront and café and even into the windows of homes. "You're some social studies teacher, Mr. Hornsby. You've even figured out a way to get a sport-playing, English-literature-loving librarian like me to fall in love with our past." But all Hornsby could do was continue to look over his shoulder.

They arrived at Quincy Market to stretches of horses and wagons with men loading and unloading goods. Suddenly, Rosie's mood changed. "Let's go back, okay? Ethan?"

"You sure?"

"Yeah. Come on, let's go."

"What's wrong, Rosie?"

"Nothing, I'm fine."

"No, you're not." Hornsby looked around to try to find whatever it was that freaked Rosie out.

"I am. I promise I am. I just want to go somewhere else."

"Not until you tell me what's going on."

"I didn't expect to be reminded, okay?"

"Of what?"

"My family and I came to Boston on a vacation when I was young. It would be our last time all together." Rosie closed her eyes. Hornsby had never seen her look so traumatized.

"Are you okay, Rosie?"

"I remember standing here at the market. My parents were fighting. It was loud. It was nonstop. I remember putting my hands over my ears."

"I'm so sorry."

"Come on, let's go."

"No," said Hornsby. "I don't know much about family problems, but I know keeping it all tucked inside isn't good."

"My father, he beat my brothers real good, Ethan. Is that what you wanted to hear?"

Hornsby felt awful. "No. That wasn't."

"He drank. It was like it took a trip to Boston to finally get my mother to show some guts. Why, Mom? Why would you let him do that to them for years? Because they weren't good enough for him at sports? Because they struggled in school when he demanded more? And you let that monster do that to them?"

"How are your brothers now?"

"Fine on the outside. Aren't we all?" Hornsby felt so awful for Rosie. He knew she needed a tight hug, but all he was able to manage was keeping his distance. "The Mizracks, huh? Perfect American family down the block, right? Sometimes, I think you not having a family was a blessing."

Hornsby had an idea. "Why don't we head over to the Parker Hotel early and sit for a hot meal. When Harding and his boys show, I'll have them pay our tab for information on the Cox campaign."

"You definitely think they'll show up?"

"I do. But I'll also make sure to hold back just enough intel for them to put us up for the night with the promise of more information in the morning."

"You're sure we can trust them?"

"No. But worst case, we take off out the side door and run our butts off back to Fenway and into our century."

All of a sudden, Hornsby heard the familiar woman's voice whisper in his ears, "You must choose."

"I just heard the voice again."

"You did?"

"Yes."

"What did she say?"

"That I must choose, whatever that's supposed to mean."

"Choose what?"

Hornsby shrugged his shoulders.

A flyer blew in the wind, landing at Rosie's feet. "Look at this. Governor Calvin Coolidge will be speaking to constituents on the radio tomorrow night."

"Then he is currently the Massachusetts governor. But none of it makes sense. If he did go into politics, then how come he only rose up to become governor but not all the way up to the presidency?"

"Ya see. Him not becoming president had nothing to do with your one day with him as a child. Maybe you should stop beating yourself up now."

Hornsby continued to wonder why his political career stopped at the governorship. "I wonder where he lives."

"Isn't there some governor's mansion or something?"

"From what I've read about Boston politics, there's no official governor's mansion. But he most likely does live in this city." Hornsby tried to add up the years in his head. "By this point, he must be fifty or close to it."

"I keep thinking about what Wells said about the Native American curse and how his people realized it was instead a blessing. I'm getting the strange intuition that it was somehow meant for you to meet both Calvin and Ben. And this will turn out to be your blessing."

All of a sudden, a police officer came from behind. "Rose Mizrack, you're under arrest. Now come with me." It was Officer Schneider.

"For what? She's done nothing wrong!" But Schneider was already pushing Rosie into the back of his police car. "What are you doing?" screamed Hornsby. "Stop this now!"

"Ethan, please help me" were the final words he heard as the car took off. Hornsby ran as fast as he could to keep up, even banged on the roof, but within seconds, the car had turned and was gone.

17

Hornsby continued his desperate race to the local police station after asking enough people for directions. He reached the counter, and a woman in front of a typewriter asked, "May I help you?"

Hornsby was hunched over the counter, huffing and puffing. "Rose Mizrack. She was just arrested and brought here." Hornsby looked around at the officers in the vicinity to see if he could pick out Officer Schneider. The attendant looked over her piles of papers.

"I have nothing on my desk about her. Do you know which officer brought her in?"

"Schneider. Officer Schneider."

"Wait here, sir."

Hornsby didn't care at this point if his death date on his tombstone would read 1919. He was going to make whatever sacrifice necessary to get Rosie back home safely. He ran his hands through his wet hair and wiped more sweat away from his brow. An Officer Schneider did approach. "That's not him. No...no...he was different. He was taller. His hair was slightly gray under the hat. Please. You have to help me. Please help me find the other Schneider."

"I'm the only Officer Schneider in this precinct."

"What was she arrested for?" the woman asked.

"He just walked up to us, cuffed her, and threw her into his car. And I just stood there. I let it happen. I allowed him to grab her. No, no, you have to help me. Please," Hornsby pleaded.

"You must choose." It was the voice again.

Hornsby looked up at the clock on the wall. It was almost seven. *Wait a minute*, he thought. Maybe Senator Harding's gang, in an attempt to gain leverage before their meeting, grabbed Rosie to extort him for all his information. He bolted out of the station and ran as fast as he could to the Parker Hotel, hearing the honks of horns as he ducked in and out of traffic.

He reached the smoke-filled cigar lobby. In the backdrop was a band playing jazz with women in dresses and tuxedoed gentleman heading in and out of the ballroom. There was a hand on his shoulder. It was Slim's. He was by himself.

Hornsby never felt this level of rage before, but it was as if each ingredient—being abandoned by his mother, Peacock trying to ruin his career, Slattery extorting him, the uncontrollable time traveling, Jeremiah getting pinned under the wagon, Calvin's lost future, and now Rosie being abducted—all came to a boil at the same time. He grabbed Slim by his collar and slammed him against the wall. "Where is she?"

"Whoa, sir! Please let go of me!" Slim begged in a gentle tone. Hornsby did let him go. "Coming here was clearly a bad idea," Slim said as he straightened out his suit.

"Tell me where she is."

"Where's who?"

"The woman I was with, the suffragette. She was abducted, and I can't find her."

"And you think we had something to do with that?"

"Who else? Now give her back," Hornsby threatened with his fist held up to Slim's nose. "You want info? I'll tell you whatever you want."

"Why don't you first back away? Then tell me what this man looked like. Maybe there's a way I can help."

"He was a Boston cop."

"Well then, sir, there's your answer. We're Ohio boys. We have nothing to do with Boston police. Now go and find some Boston boys to scream at."

Hornsby took a deep breath to try to calm down so he could begin to think more clearly. Slim was absolutely correct. There was no way these out-of-towners, just there for a baseball game, would have been involved with local police. "But… I need to find her."

Slim adjusted his shirt and suit once again. The crowd in the ballroom began to grow louder and more excited as the Charleston began. He spoke as loud as necessary. "You must understand, Senator Harding is not going to meddle into Boston police business. I wish you the best of luck finding her. Good evening now."

"Wait." Hornsby caught up to Slim. "There must be someone... just give me a name of someone in this town who could help me."

"Why don't you plead to the governor? He lives right here in Boston."

"Where? Where in Boston does he live?"

Slim looked up at the ceiling.

"He lives here in the Parker Hotel?"

"He has the penthouse. Senator Harding was just up there for a meeting about an hour ago." Slim tipped his cap. "Good luck, sir."

Hornsby ran over to the uniformed bellhop guarding the elevator. "Penthouse, please."

"That's the governor's quarters. Not without credentials."

"I was just up there."

"You were?"

"Yes. I was with Senator Harding's group. And he's sorry their meeting had to be cut short. There's just one more item he wanted me to discuss with the governor on his behalf."

"And what's your name?"

"Uh, Michael Smith."

"Wait here, Mr. Smith."

"Please, it's really important that I see him right away."

"Just wait down here." The bellhop took off upstairs in the elevator as Hornsby waited. When he returned, he said, "The governor is done entertaining for the evening."

"No...no...please. Go back up and tell him this has to do with Senator Harding wanting to ask him to be his vice president on his ticket in the next election. Go back up, please."

The bellhop returned to the elevator and rode it back upstairs. When he returned, he said, "I'm sorry, the governor will not see any more guests this evening."

Hornsby was crushed. He knew he couldn't trust the police. Someone was lying, either the first Schneider or the second. Harding and his boys wouldn't be able to assist him in a local matter, and since he was from another century, he had no family or friends to turn to.

Oh my god. It could have been the Loyalists.

Hornsby was warned by the voice, and he even had a threat taped to his classroom door. Every instinct he had told him not to bring Rosie, but he was reckless and put his best friend in danger. His poor decisions may now cost Rosie her life. "Please, sir. Just make one more trip up. Please let Governor Coolidge know that I wasn't truthful. Actually, my name isn't Smith. It's Hornsby. And I was his teacher for a day at the academy when he was twelve years old. Please remind him that we sat together along an old oak tree and talked. Please, sir. I need your help. I'm desperate for the governor's help."

"Mr. Smith, Mr. Hornsby, or whoever you are, why don't I walk over to the main desk to alert the police."

"No, please don't do that. Please. I just need to speak with Governor Coolidge."

This time, though, the bellhop held out his white-gloved hand. Hornsby reached into his pocket. "Please, God, do not look at the dates," he said to himself, placing every one of his pennies into the palm. The bellhop squeezed his fingers together, placing the coins into his pocket. "Be right back."

A few minutes later, the elevator opened. The bellhop waved in Hornsby. "He'll see me?"

"He will."

Hornsby wasn't sure why it dawned on him right at the moment he entered the elevator, but 1919 was the year Boston police attempted to form a union as they were upset with their low wages and poor working conditions. When the police commissioner refused to allow them to form a union, they went on strike for days, leading to robberies, burglaries, and looting. This event propelled Governor Calvin Coolidge to the White House as he gained a national reputation for supporting public safety and security after stepping in to take control of the police, forcing both an end to the strike and the riots. But Hornsby also realized what this meant—at this point in time—if the cops are at odds with the police commissioner, then they are also at odds with Calvin.

Hornsby was expecting the elevator to open to a hallway, but instead, it opened right up to Calvin's living room. The governor was standing right there next to his wife. He was in a green sweater with silver dress pants. His hair was greased over to the side. Hornsby found it hard to believe that just a couple of days ago, he was talking with Calvin, the child, and now Calvin, the governor, was married with children. One of them peeked out from his bedroom. Hornsby wondered if he was the one who would die at age sixteen in 1924 of a toe infection, something that today would be easily treatable.

There was total silence. Hornsby was reminded that the only person on Earth more uncomfortable in a social situation than him was Silent Cal. The bellhop exited. "I'm sorry for lying to you, Governor. I should've realized that getting a political edge would never be your priority."

But Calvin still said nothing. To not even offer a greeting was extreme, even for Silent Cal. But then Mrs. Coolidge spoke up, "So you're the famous Mr. Hornsby, the mysterious teacher who, in only one day, has had a lifetime effect on my husband, only to vanish forever. We tried to track you down. And this evening, you show up out of nowhere with stories about working for Senator Harding. Who are you really, sir?"

"I'm really me. Mr. Ethan Hornsby, the teacher who listened to the governor's thoughtful speech about his mother."

"And looking just about the same as I remember," Cal finally said.

"Good genetics, I guess." Hornsby realized they had no idea what that meant. Hornsby moved closer to Calvin and offered his hand. Calvin gently shook it. "I'm so sorry. I wanted to be there for you longer than just one day. Trust me, I wanted to come back."

"Then why didn't you?" asked Calvin.

For some reason, Hornsby felt comfortable enough to be honest. "I didn't know how to come back."

"Please sit down, Mr. Hornsby," Calvin said. "Can I offer you a drink?"

"No, thank you." Hornsby took a moment to reflect on Calvin's life and how history taught that he never veered from his principles and values. When he took over as president, he cleaned up Harding's corruption. And he was so thankful if you supported him, he didn't take any of his constituents for granted. "I thought I screwed you up, Governor."

"Screwed me up?"

"I thought I overstepped my boundaries. I thought maybe... I changed the course of your life in a negative, harmful way."

"My life has been a challenge, much like everybody. But one must dedicate oneself and work hard at what they do. And you helped me quite a bit, Mr. Hornsby. That was a very difficult time for me. My other teachers had no compassion. They never seemed to understand me the way you did, within only a few hours. Whenever it's time for me to give a speech and I become nervous, I always think back to that afternoon by the tree."

Hornsby felt such warmth in his heart. He was living the dream of every teacher, which is to have a positive impact on a student. Of course, this was one unorthodox way to leave his mark. But if *he* didn't screw up Calvin Coolidge, why then doesn't the governor still go on to become president?

"I wish I had more time to catch up with you, Governor, but the truth is I reached out to you this evening because a corrupt cop unlawfully arrested my friend. And I don't know how else I could get her back without your help."

"Which officer?"

"Schneider."

"Do you have any idea why?"

"For no reason."

"Did you check in with the station?"

Hornsby was getting agitated with the slow-talking Cal but tried to keep it from showing. "I went through all the proper channels. And here I am."

"I pride myself on not doing favors for friends."

"This isn't a favor. This is a young girl arrested for no reason by a corrupt officer."

"Okay, Mr. Hornsby. Fortunately, at the current time, my police commissioner is on great speaking terms with the police chief and the department. He has decided to allow them to form their union chapter."

He has?

"I have talked some sense into him."

You have?

Hornsby said, "But I thought Commissioner Curtis swore he would never allow them to form a union?"

"Let's just say, he's come around to the idea. And by the end of the summer, I suspect there's a terrific chance that I and Mrs. Coolidge, along with Commissioner Curtis and the police chief, will be holding a press conference to announce the news of their new union chapter."

Hornsby was stunned. So this was why Coolidge isn't nominated for the Harding ticket. Without the angry police strike and without Coolidge showing his leadership skills and standing up for public safety, he'll never gain the national recognition. Governor of Massachusetts is as far as his political career would ever go.

"I'll get the police commissioner on the phone for you. Let's find out what happened to your friend."

"You must choose," whispered the voice.

Hornsby now understood his choices:

1. Alert Calvin that he should force the police commissioner to call off all negotiations with the police right away. The famous Boston Police Strike of 1919 would still happen. Coolidge would become vice president and then president, returning the Roaring Twenties to the history books. This would also mean that an upset police chief and the department may never help him find Rosie.
2. Keep his mouth shut. The police would get their union. There would never be a strike or a Coolidge presidency, and there would be a longer Great Depression. But the police would remain an ally, helping him to find Rosie.

Rescue history or rescue Rosie?

This was easy. Hornsby kept his mouth shut as Calvin walked into his office to use the phone. He returned shortly after though with devastating news. "There's no Rose Mizrack in custody. Whoever took her was not police."

"Please, I still need their help to find her."

"I provided them with your description. They'll be out there looking for her. I'd hate to make a promise I couldn't keep."

Hornsby's heart was broken, his energy gone. He thanked Calvin and his wife and rang for the elevator. He exited the elevator, walked through the noisy lobby, and out into the street. He walked and walked, block by block, searching for her, but it was frighteningly dark now on most corners. Every now and then, the lights from a car would help, but he just kept going. He followed the lights from ships down to Boston Harbor. He walked through Southend, calling her name, made his way through Dorchester, looking at every passing face, asking if anyone had seen an auburn-haired woman with a white brimmed hat and a purple, flowery dress. He labored through Roxbury on whatever fumes of energy he had left.

He could sense he was now being followed. It happened in a back alley in Roxbury. He was jumped, punched to the ground, and robbed. The assailants left him for dead. He lay on the dirty pavement, feeling as if he deserved every bit of it.

18

When he awoke to daylight, he could barely move. His sneakers were gone. He felt large swelling around his right eye and a giant bump on his head. His right elbow was killing him. He could not locate his glasses. They were more than likely broken anyway.

He continued his trek, now barefoot and sore, his eyes squinting, trying to make out any familiar landmark he could find within the bustling city. He continued to call out for Rosie, reaching into his pocket for his phone out of habit. He wished he could check his text messages. He would do anything just to be able to call her to hear her voice. He sat down on an empty bench, completely demoralized. He looked down at the cuts on his feet.

It finally dawned on him.

Not only was Officer Schneider not wearing the correct leather boots of a 1919 Boston police officer, but he was also wearing shoes that had to come from a future era.

Suddenly, Hornsby felt a boost of adrenaline. He walked as fast as he could, even with all the pain of stepping on pebbles, nails, and pieces of glass. He managed to locate the entrance to Fenway Park.

There was only one man who could explain this.

*****

Bang, bang.

Hornsby hammered his fist against the door to Jim Well's antique store. Wells signaled with his hand that he was coming, but Hornsby kept angrily banging anyway.

"I don't open for another hour."

"Am I talking to you or your fake self?"

Wells took a look at all the marks on Hornsby's face and his bare feet. "You didn't even go home first?"

"So you do know what the hell is going on."

"Of course, I do. Now come on in and meet Lou. And how about I make you a fresh cup of coffee?"

"Mr. Wells, Rosie is missing in the year 1919. Whatever you know about who took her, you better start talking." But Wells didn't get the chance to answer. The fragile Lou Boyd came out from the back office and was leaning on his cane in the middle of the carpet. "I feel like I'm looking at your father."

"You knew my father?"

"I knew him well, Ethan. He was a fine man, was willing to do anything for your mom and our colony." Lou caned over and gave Ethan a soft kiss on his cheek. "You look just like him."

"Well, I only want to speak with Mr. Wells."

"It's all right. I already know the questions you'll be asking," said the elder Lou. "And I understand how you must be feeling about all this."

"Where is Rosie, Mr. Wells?"

"She's home safe."

"She's home?"

"Please, Ethan," Wells said. "Let's go into my office and sit down to talk. I'll explain everything."

"How could you? I'll never forgive you for making Rosie some chess piece in whatever game you're playing."

"This is not a game, son. This is war," Lou stated.

"War with who?"

"The Loyalists."

Hornsby looked at both Lou and Wells. "You know about the Loyalists?"

"Please, Ethan. Let's sit down. There is much to discuss."

"Actually, I don't want to hear another word of any of this craziness. You say Rosie is home safe? Then that's where I'm going. After that, I have an event to attend on the school campus, bloody faced and all."

"You're not leaving yet," said Wells, who moved in front of the door.

"Oh, I see. The thief who travels back in time to steal all these antiques is now going to tell me when I can leave."

"You learned firsthand that you couldn't bring anything back with you."

"I'm sure you figured it out somehow. It can't be a coincidence that you're an antiques dealer."

"Yes, I use time traveling to my advantage. Unbeknownst to others, I've traveled back to learn the real history of items and traced their official origins. This has made me very valuable in the industry. Unlike other dealers, I'm also able to authenticate artifacts without being conned into fakes. But a thief? That I am not."

"Okay, but you admit you use time traveling to your advantage."

"As will you, Ethan. There'll be no stopping your power once you learn to control it."

"Is that why you stepped up to take care of me? Bought the house? Just so you can use me later over some powers?"

Wells appeared saddened. "No, Ethan. That is not why."

Lou ended the awkwardness. "Please, Ethan, there's no more time to waste. As you know, the country is being robbed of the Roaring Twenties."

"Please, just let me exit, Mr. Wells."

"Not before you hear us out. It's in your best interests to learn about the Loyalists."

"How would you know about my best interests? You people are nothing but a bunch of colonists who don't belong here."

"You're right, we don't belong here," responded Lou. "But this country has afforded us lives we could never have dreamed of. Jim and I would do anything to help this great nation."

"But there haven't been Loyalists since the Revolutionary War era. Why would anyone be loyal to England these days?"

"Remember, Ethan," said Wells, "those of us from Roanoke have English blood. Our families were all loyal to the king of England.

Imagine the reaction when we arrived in 1987 to learn this was now the United States."

"Okay, so?"

Lou said, "Some of us never accepted it. Still won't. There's a faction from our group who still believe this land should belong to the mother country. These Loyalists have been using their powers to travel back in time to alter history. Canceling the Roaring Twenties and extending the Great Depression is just their latest attack. You should have seen how close they came to ensuring that the South won the Civil War. The United States we know and love today would've never existed had that happened."

"Then they are trying to ruin our country?"

"Yes, they think by altering the history of the United States, the nation will at some point fall. They truly hate that this land is no longer England's."

"Then what is it you guys do?"

"We travel back in time to fix it."

"No offense, Lou," Hornsby said, "but you're too old to walk without a cane. You want me to believe you're still capable of time traveling?"

"You're right, I'm no longer able. But there are others in our group that Jim and I want you to meet. They were once children in our colony and now only a few years older than you. Think of our group as the Sons of Liberty. The original Sons were a group of patriots who acted to ensure that the United States would have its independence. Now our little group of patriots is only trying to make sure that our country's history remains as it was originally written. But if the Loyalists are allowed to eliminate the prosperous times, if they are able to wipe out civil rights, if they can bring more corruption to government, they'll get their wish, and at some point, in the past, the United States will have been overthrown."

Wells added, "We believe their attempt to get to and alter young Benjamin Harrison's life is only the first part of a multiphase attack on civil rights in this country. We've gathered intelligence that the next target of their civil rights attack is Frederick Douglass, the former slave turned civil rights leader. Then they'll keep going."

"You mean keep going to Martin Luther King's time?"

"Yes. If the Loyalists are allowed to complete their mission, the world will have never heard of Martin Luther King Jr."

"I'm not sure I would want to live in this country if there was never Martin Luther King."

"That's exactly what the Loyalists are hoping for," said Wells.

Lou added, "Do you understand now our sense of urgency? And we're going to need your help next with Frederick Douglass. We need you to travel back in time to wait by a train. The Loyalists are going to try to keep Douglass from escaping his master and getting on that train to New York. If they are successful, history will have never heard of Frederick Douglass."

"But you must know already, I've made nothing but mistakes. I might have gotten Benjamin Harrison's friend Jeremiah killed."

"No, you didn't. Read your updated history closely. Harrison's talked about the time he saved Jeremiah's life and the impact it had on him. You did that."

"I did?"

"You did. You did very well, Ethan, to make sure Benjamin Harrison remained an early advocate for the civil rights of blacks and a natural conservationist."

"What exactly were the Loyalists doing to Ben?"

"Their strategy is to place people back in time to impact change. We believe a Loyalist traveled back and weaved into Mrs. Harrison's circle of friends. Each day at church, he spoke to her, filling her head with nonsense that Jeremiah was dangerous for her son and that the boys should be kept away from each other. But you countered."

"But I didn't know what I was doing or why I even wound up there. And it seems like you guys have been doing just fine without me. Honestly, all I want to do is teach kids from today, not the 1800s."

Lou lifted up his cane. "You already pointed out. I can't do it anymore. And Jim over here, even keeping himself in tip-top shape, will eventually lose the battle to Father Time."

"Can't you people have time-traveling kids or something?"

"No birth has proven to extend the power. Except for you, conceived at Roanoke."

Hornsby thought about the Loyalists traveling back in time to impact change and then about Calvin. He was never supposed to be allowing the police to have their own union chapter. "It must've been the Loyalists who planted people inside the negotiations between the police and Coolidge. That's why there was no strike, and Coolidge never reached the White House."

"Which was why it was critically important for you, with your access to Coolidge, to fix it," said a disappointed Wells.

"You kidnapped Rosie knowing it would send me right to him." Wells didn't respond. "Who was Officer Schneider really? Another one of your Sons of Liberty thugs?"

"You had your chance with Coolidge, and you never did what you were supposed to!" Wells barked back.

"Because I had to put my friend first. I can't believe you don't understand that. If you want to make me your puppet, that's one thing, but leave Rosie out of this. Wait a minute. That's exactly what you wanted to happen. You did this so that I would never even consider bringing her along again."

"I just wanted you to see that she's a liability."

"Was it you who also left that note on my classroom door about the Loyalists?"

Wells and Lou looked at each other. "No, that wasn't us. Clearly, your time-traveling powers have gotten more than just our attention."

"Well, I'm not some savage colonist like you people, caught up in some whacked-out war. And between Mrs. Harrison's shotgun and getting mugged in an ally in Boston, I'm lucky to even be alive."

"You took unnecessary risks," said Lou. "Jim and I intend to train you properly."

"And there's still time for you to send Coolidge to the White House," said Wells.

"Why don't you fix it?"

"Because the rest of us don't have the access that you have to him. You have become our best chance. There was a reason why you were sent first to his childhood. You now have a lifelong bond."

"How can you see me?"

"Feel would be the better word. Remember the connection to nature I told you about?"

Hornsby looked at each of them. "Then it was you guys who were controlling my journeys?"

Wells and Lou shook their heads. "We're not the ones in control."

"Well, you and the Loyalists won't have to worry about me anymore because I'm done time traveling. Even if that means giving up a career as a teacher." Hornsby walked past Wells to the doorway. "Now I have to go keep a promise that I'd help at a cancer fundraiser."

"Before you drive away, I have something to give you, Ethan." Wells walked to his office and came out with a small key.

"What's this?"

"It's the key to the missing section."

19

Hornsby's first stop was, of course, Rosie's. She opened the door with monumental relief and a giant hug. "I was so worried about you, Ethan. My god, your eye! And your pants are torn! What happened to your sneakers?"

Hornsby wanted to tell her all about how he put his life on the line to find her but only said, "I'm just glad you're okay."

"Please, Ethan, come inside right away."

"I can't."

"Why not?"

"I just can't."

"I'm so sorry, Ethan. I tried to get back to you. I didn't know how. And there was no way to reach you with a message. I begged Jim Wells to take me back, but he clearly had other intentions."

"What did they tell you about all this?"

"Nothing. They wouldn't tell me anything."

"Then let's leave it at that."

"Leave it at what?"

"I'm just sorry for putting you in danger. I should have listened to my gut and never brought you. And I'll never make that mistake again."

"No, Ethan, I'm now part of this. Tell me what you know about Wells and his gang."

"I don't know anything."

"You're a terrible liar." Rosie placed her fingers softly onto Hornsby's swollen eye. "And you don't deserve any of what you're going through. But we can't make it stop until you tell me everything. I saw it in them, Ethan. They're up to something. And they're not like you and me. They're still brutes from another time period."

"How did they get you home?"

"The one dressed like the cop took me through his portal near Quincy Market."

"Well, I'm glad you're home safe. That's all that's important."

"I'm part of this, Ethan, and I'm not going to let you shut me out."

"No, Rosie, you're not part of anything. I don't want you getting into trouble at work for me. And the last thing I ever want to see again is what happened to you in Boston. I learned a hard lesson."

"But seeing Fenway Park, walking around Boston with you in 1919"—Rosie's eyes became watery—"it was the most memorable thing I've ever done." She held her hands up. "And I'm not hurt. I'm fine."

"Goodbye, Rosie."

"No, Ethan."

"Yes, Rosie. And if it takes us not speaking anymore just to get through to you, then I'm prepared for that consequence."

"Where are you going?"

"Home for a much-needed shower. Relay for Life starts in an hour."

"How are you going to explain the black eye?"

"It's easier than having to explain not showing up."

Hornsby took off in his car. Never before in his adult life had he needed his mother more. He thought about the day a dejected Mr. Wells returned after another day of searching and said, "There's a very good chance we may never find her."

He continued to examine the small key that Wells handed him. One side had a number. The other said Chase Bank. He entered his lonely, cold house and cleaned himself up, stuffing his painfully sore, swollen feet into an old pair of sneakers before driving back to school. He finally found a parking spot among the growing crowd, but before heading up to the field, he had one more stop to make.

The building was empty and quiet. Hornsby looked up at one of the many cameras that hung from the ceiling. If someone asked, he would tell them he was looking for Mrs. Peacock to discuss another way he could volunteer around the school. It would be a total lie, but at least, he would have some semblance of an alibi for what he was about to do.

He made his way down the hallway to the main entrance of the building where the nurse, attendance office, a conference room for parent meetings, and the office of the big bird, Mrs. Peacock, connected in a circle. Peacock's office, though, actually turned out to be further down a large corridor, once you opened what appeared to be her door. That's what was so tricky. Anything could go wrong down this corridor.

He stealthily opened her door and crept down the corridor, passing empty offices, only to reach Martha's office, who was Peacock's assistant. Martha's office was adjacent to Peacock's larger office, which was wide enough to hold an entire round table of teachers, plus a desk and a couch. Luckily, no one was around.

Hornsby peeked into Peacock's office. Over on her extensive mahogany desk, there was one neat pile of papers and many pictures. There were even pictures on the wall shelves and on the windowsill. But it would only be possible for her to have family and friends if she were actually a human being.

Hornsby stood in the doorway, scared to death of someone suddenly appearing. This darn corridor. There was only one way out.

He continued to wonder why Peacock was in the library, asking about the Lost Colony of Roanoke. "What are you up to, Peacock?"

It is now or never, Hornsby thought. *Just get in and out.* He marched straight for her desk. He quickly made his way through the pile, but it was only papers about students. He opened the top drawer to find the usuals: gum, tape, a scissor, and a bunch of pens.

He leaned down to open the other drawers. Files. Each was labeled with the names of either students or teachers. He did a quick scan to see if his name was atop any, but Peacock wouldn't think he was even worth the ink. He sat down in the chair and wheeled over to the computer. He tapped the keyboard, but it was password protected.

Then a photo on the left of the computer caught his eye. It was Peacock as a younger woman, standing with three boys who looked like her sons. He lifted it up to bring it closer to his eyes. He had seen this exact photo before but couldn't recall where. On the other side of the computer was a book titled *Benjamin Harrison* written by Charles Calhoun.

"Mr. Hornsby, may I help you with something?" Hornsby's heart stopped. It was Peacock.

Hornsby held up the book. "I didn't know you were a fan of history, Mrs. Peacock."

"Was I supposed to tell you?"

Hornsby examined the book. "And Benjamin Harrison, one of the least talked about presidents. I'm surprised you would find an interest." Hornsby looked around some more. "Might you also have a book about Calvin Coolidge?"

"Since you're interested, I happen to be reading the entire presidential series, and I'm currently on Harrison, number twenty-three. But when I reach Coolidge, I'll be sure to let you know. Shall I also turn in a report to you?"

"I don't think that will be necessary." Hornsby continued to wonder about that first time he traveled to meet Calvin and why Peacock, unlike all the others, did not see his fake self and how she was able to interrupt his travel just by entering the room. "By the way, Mrs. Peacock, you wouldn't happen to know anything about this, would you?" Hornsby handed her the flyer about the Loyalists.

"Why would I?"

"Aren't you the principal here? I thought it was your job to know everything that happens. This seems to have been printed with paper and ink from the building's copier."

"Well, I wasn't aware of it."

Hornsby gestured. "Please keep the flyer as a souvenir."

"You know, Mr. Hornsby, being in my office without my consent, that's a fireable offense. But going through my drawers? Now that's a criminal act."

"But I'll claim I was only innocently here to meet with you. And here you are. How convenient." Hornsby peeked out of the office.

"I don't see any witnesses, so let's have our meeting. I just learned that my mother time traveled from a lost colony. Isn't that really crazy?" Peacock said nothing. "And get this, there were also eight other women in that colony. You wouldn't happen to know anything about them, would you?"

"I wouldn't. And I want you out of my office. Now!"

"Let's see, there was Dorothy Bradford, there was Miriam Walters, there was Grace Jones… I can't recall the rest of them, but I could only imagine what it must have felt like for a time-traveling woman from the 1500s to suddenly be living in 1987. One day, you don't even have the right to own property, and the next, the world is your oyster. I'm guessing you… I mean *these*…women would have loved that they could now vote, attend college, and have careers outside the home. Am I right, Mrs. Peacock?"

"If you don't leave now, I'm calling security."

Hornsby took a picture from the desk and showed it to Peacock. "Can you produce a photo of yourself from before 1987? Because I don't think you can. I've searched and searched all over the Internet for information about your life, any photo of your childhood that would've been shared on social media—a birth certificate, anything that would disprove my theory about you. But there isn't anything to be found, is there?"

Peacock stepped in closer to Hornsby. "You always thought you were the smartest kid in class, didn't you?"

"Actually, if you must know, I had no confidence in myself at all."

"Get. Out. Of. My. Office."

Hornsby showcased the Harrison book again. "Can I keep this? I can't seem to find my own copy. By the way, his mother, a terrible shot."

"Get out!" Peacock screamed with such aggression. Hornsby learned she had actually been wearing a wig all these years as it shifted.

On his way out the door, Hornsby made sure Peacock saw him dump the Harrison book into the garbage.

He exited the building as quickly as possible and made his way up the field to find Mrs. Baker. "Oh my god, Ethan! What happened to you?"

"Long story."

*****

Hornsby wasn't planning on staying long. He remained at his post near the bleachers until everything was clearly under control. It was mostly an adult crowd anyway, and there were more teachers helping than Mrs. Baker led on. He fulfilled his mission, show Mrs. Baker that he was here then how hurt he was. That would be his excuse to bail early. He dipped out through the side fence into a neighborhood and walked the long way back to his car. No one even noticed. More importantly, he only had a half hour left before Chase Bank closed since it was Saturday.

A teller led him down the hallway and then down a flight of stairs to a large vault of safety deposit boxes. He looked around at the numbers and finally found a match to the key. He opened it. Inside was a bunch of old handwritten pages—*the missing section of the Pierce journal.* Hornsby practically tripped on the steps, almost walked into a wall, and then nearly banged into two customers while trying to read it during his way out to the parking lot.

This section was from 1987 on. His mother must have kept it locked up because it served as proof of their time travel. The first few pages described the difficult early days in the church, which corroborated Well's stories with the very helpful priest. But then the next section was about his mother's joy when he was born and details of her hospital stay. The very last of it was about him as a baby. But that was it. "Where's the rest, Mom?"

But then he noticed a small piece of paper clipped to the last page. It was also his mother's handwriting.

Ethan, if you have received this key from Jim, it means that you connected my two worlds and you know the truth. I am writing this note to you because I have to go away now. Just know that I will always be thinking of you. Please grow to be the man I always envisioned you to become. Live your dreams. Be strong, my boy. I can never forget you.

Hornsby dropped the papers. His hands were shaking, tears flowing down his face. He tried to make sense of it. This confirmed she was alive. It confirmed she knew she was leaving. It also confirmed that she knew she would never be coming home.

But why, Mom? Why would you do this to me?

He somehow arrived home after driving through blurry, watery eyes. He went to the refrigerator out of habit but couldn't even think about food. He took at least a few bites of some frozen pizza to keep from throwing up from starvation, placed his face into a pillow, and cried himself to sleep to the sounds of Rosie's repeated phone calls and texts.

Before the sun could rise, his head popped up from the pillow. His eyes were open wide. He couldn't believe he hadn't seen it right away.

He needed to get to Jim Wells immediately.

And for the first time, he had a feeling in his body that connected them. He could feel that Wells was back in 1919.

20

Hornsby, wearing his turn-of-the-century work cap, stood outside the same Boston police station, where he went searching for Rosie, just two days earlier. In his hand, he held a stack of flyers, printed out on school paper using school ink from a school machine, another fireable offense since it was forbidden to use these materials for personal use. That he was able to place himself back to the exact time and place he wanted meant he was getting closer to gaining control of his traveling, and yet he was feeling the opposite of harmonious and balanced. This new information about his mother steered him onto an emotional roller coaster.

He looked down at the flyers. One side said, "Commissioner Curtis Refuses to Meet. Time to Protest in the Street!" The other side said, "Commissioner Curtis Won't Listen. Make Our Protest Glisten!"

Hornsby was going to try to fool an entire police department into thinking they needed to strike. The strike would allow Calvin to show his leadership ability by standing up for public safety, which will draw national attention and earn him the vice presidency under Warren Harding. It was now or never for the Roaring Twenties.

"You're gonna need this." It was Wells dressed as an officer. In his hand was a uniform for Hornsby.

"How did you know I would be coming?"

"Because I could feel it. You've never stopped caring about Coolidge's future or our nation's history."

"All these years, I went to bed, thinking my mother didn't love me. And the whole time, you had that key."

"How was I supposed to explain any of this to a kid? It had to happen only when you were ready."

"You're not the judge and jury of when I'm ready."

"I'm sorry, Ethan. I made a decision to protect you."

"And how exactly were you protecting me?"

"Think about if this information wound up in your hands when you were younger, and you slipped and told a teacher or the police... you would have wound up in front of a psychologist and then sent away to a special school."

"But my mother is alive! And you gave up on her."

That angered Wells, "I've never given up on her!"

"You told me my mother couldn't time travel."

"She can't."

"Which was why I never considered that she would have still wound up in another time and place. I never even considered the possibility that someone would bring her with them. Tell me, Mr. Wells, how many times did you bring her with you?" Wells looked away. "And the reason the police could never track her down is that she's not in the present day. She never did abandon me. She was banished."

"I'm afraid she was."

"But by who? Who would force her to another time as punishment? Wait...the Loyalists did this?"

"I'm afraid they did."

"And you've done nothing to stop them?"

Wells tried to calm Hornsby down. "This is a very complicated situation."

"Because it's not *your* mother. She knew it was going to happen. Why didn't you protect her?"

"Because her focus was you, Ethan. She asked me to protect you. It was a deal she was forced to take." Hornsby looked away. "I'm so sorry you've had to go through all this. I really am. But I was following your mother's wishes."

"There has to be more to it, Mr. Wells." Hornsby looked him up and down. "And I'm going to find out why you've done nothing to the Loyalists."

Wells grabbed the flyers out of Hornsby's hand. "Time to focus on why we're here."

"I'm sorry, but I'll be operating alone."

"You will learn, when part of the Sons of Liberty, we work only as a team."

"I thought I've made it clear, I'm part of nothing." Hornsby took back the flyers. "Now if you'll excuse me, I need to hand these out."

Wells stepped in front of him. "Please. Let me help."

Hornsby hesitated but then looked over at the station, thinking about what this moment meant to history. "Okay, take half. You hit all the blocks up in that area, get to all the cops working the beat. Then head down those blocks over there. I'll go that way. We need to both be preaching the same message. If the commissioner won't grant us our union chapter, then our voices must be heard. Tell every cop you see we will be gathering here on Main Street right away. The strike begins now! Let's go!"

Hornsby found a spot in between buildings where he could quickly get changed into the uniform. The pants were a bit tight and short, and the cap could only make it over about three-quarters of his head, but he leaned the brim up a bit to make it work and let the belt buckle remain loose under the coat. He did his best to brush away as much lint and as many wrinkles as he could with his hands. He continued to reflect, wondering why the Loyalists would see a simple restaurant manager and single mom as some threat needing to be banished.

Hornsby made his way around town, handing out flyers to officers. "Okay, show some confidence, Mr. Hornsby," he told himself. "You look the part. Now you just have to act it."

He entered the police station.

But, of course, it was the same woman who was at the front desk the last time he was in there pleading for Rosie. He made sure not to make eye contact and reminded himself that the uniform afforded him all the authority he would need. He checked out the room. There were about twenty police officers, either sitting or standing and about a dozen women working at desks. And there was enough smoke from cigarettes to make him want to call the fire department.

He handed out the rest of the flyers. "May I have everyone's attention? Hello, may I have everyone's attention, please?" The officers eventually quieted down. Everyone was staring. "My name is Harvey, uh, um, Bishop, and I am from a, uh, from a nearby precinct." Hornsby wondered if he looked too ridiculous in his ill-fitting uniform to be taken seriously. Plus, the swelling around his eye was now in the violet-yellow-green multicolor phase. But he continued to think about Calvin and how important it was for him to reach the White House. "We have all been set up by Commissioner Curtis. He will not be allowing us to form a union, after all. It was all lies!" Hornsby allowed the officers a few minutes of commotion. Then he added, "We will not be getting paid as much as he promised, and he will continue to force us to work long hours. Commissioner Curtis just doesn't care about us!" There was now a real buzz in the room. "As you see from the flyer, the strike is happening now. I need everyone to stop what they're doing and join me on Main Street."

"What strike? I see nothing!" shouted one of the officers who peeked out of a window. Hornsby walked over to the window. *Oh no.* None of the officers had begun to gather. *Please, Mr. Wells, come through.*

If there was ever a time to get down on his knees and pray, Hornsby thought, it was now. If the police didn't begin to gather on Main Street, these cops would clearly see him as a hoax, and he would be locked up. A few officers headed for the door, checking the street.

"What is this, a joke?"

"Looks like a joke to me."

"Who are you really?"

"Yeah, what's going on here?"

The real Officer Schneider approached. "I know you from somewhere."

"Me? Uh, maybe from one of our police Christmas parties or something."

Schneider just continued to stare.

Hornsby desperately made one last attempt. "Please, everyone, join me on Main Street. There's going to be a strike, and we need to support our fellow officers!"

"You're a phony!"

"Yeah, you're no cop!"

"Arrest him!"

Just then, Officer Schneider remembered and said, "You're that man who was in here looking for his girlfriend." He grabbed Hornsby by the arm and began to lead him to a jail cell.

"Let go of me," Hornsby pleaded.

"I'm booking you for the night for impersonating an officer. Now get in there." Schneider shoved Hornsby into the cell.

But before he had the chance to lock the cell door, Wells practically kicked the front door of the police station open. "It's a strike!" He pointed. Behind him, on Main Street, were about fifty police officers.

"Look, there really is a strike!" another officer shouted out.

"Yeah, he was telling the truth. It's a strike. Let's go, boys!" said another. Within seconds, it looked like a sea of dark blue. Hornsby knelt down, but it was not to pray or say thanks. It was to catch his breath.

Standing over him was Mr. Wells. "You okay?"

Hornsby stood up and shook Well's hand. "Thank you."

*****

Hornsby ran back over to his changing area and quickly threw on his old clothes. He then darted for the Parker Hotel. He covertly waited by the front desk. There he comes. It was Calvin exiting the elevator to two men who were waiting for him. "What is happening here, Mr. Curtis?" Hornsby overheard Coolidge asking, which meant one of them was Commissioner Curtis.

"Riots, looting, theft. We're losing control of our city."

"Well, it's your job to get control of it!" demanded Calvin.

"There's nothing I can do about that." Curtis pointed to the streets, showing Calvin the chaos and the miles of police who were doing nothing to tame it.

"But why?"

"It must be because of this." Curtis showed Calvin the flyer.

"But this isn't true!"

"It doesn't matter now. My officers seem to believe it."

"Make them listen to you!"

"I can't, Governor. It's too late."

Hornsby listened carefully as Calvin finally said the words that would give them back the Roaring Twenties, "Then I have no choice but to take control of the city in the name of public safety! I will run the police department myself if that's what it will take. Set up a meeting with the police chief. I will put an end to all the chaos, once and for all!"

This was the reaction Hornsby was hoping for. He watched as Calvin and Curtis stepped into a Ford bound for city hall. Meanwhile, the third man took off in another direction. Hornsby took one last look at the Ford as it drove away. "The White House can't wait for all your practical jokes and wonderful speeches, Calvin." Hornsby tipped his cap. "Good luck, sir."

He then took off into a jog as he shifted his focus to the mysterious third man, who was about six feet tall and had blond hair. The man was waiting at the corner for traffic to subside. "Why didn't you go with them to the city hall?"

The blond man turned. Hornsby could see it in his piercing blue eyes that he recognized him. "Move along before you get hurt again."

It was the picture of Peacock with her children that tipped him off. Now one of her sons was standing in front of him in 1919. "You're a Loyalist. And I just foiled your plans."

"The name is Bart. And nothing is ever foiled, Hornsby."

"Are you sure about that, Bart? Both Coolidge and Harrison are back where they belong in the history books."

Bart moved in closer. "The great chef never just cooks one dish. He also makes sure there are plenty of other dishes to serve, just in case."

"Tell me where my mother is."

Bart, the Loyalist, laughed. "You're barking up the wrong tree with that one."

"Tell me, goddamn it."

"You really don't know, do you?"

"Know what?"

"The only person left who knows your mother's exact whereabouts is your principal and my mother."

Hornsby was shell-shocked. So this was the reason why Wells wasn't tougher on the Loyalists. Peacock is holding the most important bargaining chip. He could barely catch his breath as he watched Bart the Loyalist cross the street and disappear into his portal.

He made his way slowly back through the crowds, trying to keep from being hit with flying debris or stuck in between rowdy mobs. He finally reached the entrance of Fenway Park. Wells was there waiting. "I'm heading further back to 1838 to join the others and make sure runaway slave Frederick Douglass gets on a train to New York. We must make sure he becomes a civil rights leader."

"I'm going home."

"I can use your help."

"Mr. Wells, I just found out, from a Loyalist no less, that my boss is the one person on Earth who can tell me where my mother is. She also happens to spend her days trying to make my life as miserable as possible. And let me add, she just busted me robbing her office."

"She was Dorothy Bradford in the colony. And let me guess, she just happened to show up at her office right in time."

"She did."

"As I've told you, we're all connected in a different way through nature. You can become powerful enough to stop all of it. But only when you join us for good." Wells took out a black-and-white photo of his mother from his wallet. It was slightly torn around the edges. "Take this for now."

"Where did you get this?"

"I took a negative I had of her and had it printed in black and white so I could carry it with me to the old times to search for her."

"But why, Mr. Wells? Why did they see her as a threat?"

"Find her. She will answer that herself. Now I have a train to catch."

Hornsby watched Wells leave and continued his walk into Fenway Park and his portal but then heard the voice in his ear again. He couldn't believe he hadn't realized it earlier, but it was his mother's voice all along. "I'm why you love history," she whispered. Hornsby immediately had flashbacks of being a young child on her lap, his mother reading all about American history to him, pointing out the important people and events. He thought about what Wells said, *"As I've told you, we're all connected in a different way through nature."*

"Tell me where you are, Mom."

"I can't."

"Why not? Please come home. I need you."

But there was no response. Now Hornsby thought about the moment in the antique shop when he questioned if Wells had been controlling his journeys. But had it been his mother who's really been in control?

Where are you, Mom? And why?

Then he felt anxiety about having to face his colonial Loyalist principal and his rival Mr. Slattery in the morning, while also feeling heartbroken about losing his friend Rosie. "I can't do it, Mom. I can't face any of it. I'm not strong enough."

The voice appeared again. "What has history taught you?"

Hornsby thought it over. "That it doesn't matter when you lived. The worst place to be is alone." He paused. "And that's where I am."

"I suffered through a starving winter. I lost your father."

"That must have been so hard. How did you endure it?"

"You tell me what did I do?"

"You took care of me."

"And what should you be doing?"

"It's so confusing. Mr. Wells wants me to join his gang to try to fix history. But I don't want that."

"Then what is it you want?"

"I've only wanted to become a great teacher at Upper Kakapo. It's just everything else gets in the way."

"Are you sure about that?"

Hornsby tried to understand what she meant. "But how can I teach when I keep getting sent back in time? How can I get a job when my principal banished you and now wants to do the same to me?"

"I asked you what did I do to endure it, the starving winter, losing your father, but you answered, 'By taking care of me.' But that's not what I did."

"What do you mean?"

"What I did was I found the confidence within myself. Only then could I create a life for us."

"But I've had so many years alone. I don't think I can ever find confidence in myself. I needed you. I needed your voice. You weren't there."

Hornsby could hear crying. "Think clearly, Ethan. What would have happened to Calvin and Ben if you didn't come along?"

"I don't know. How am I supposed to know that?"

"Think."

"I guess history would have been different. But so what? Coolidge and Harrison are not on anyone's list of most important presidents."

"Then you weren't put in front of them for history, were you?"

"They were troubled. They needed help."

"And you did your best to help them because you already have inside what you need. You already know that helping students is what must come first, even if it means risking everything."

"But, Mom…"

"I've got to go now, Ethan. When it is necessary, you will hear my voice again."

"I'm gonna find you, Mom. I promise. I'm never going to stop looking."

21

Hornsby awoke with a renewed appetite and drove for a monster-sized McDonald's breakfast. He could hear Mr. Slattery's voice demanding that his Monday morning coffee should have extra sugar, but he didn't buy one.

He entered the school fashionably late.

This morning, his assignment was to continue to sub for Ms. Shaw, joining Ms. Bean and her wonderful group of special education students once again. But this time, Hornsby entered the room glowing with confidence. "Hello again, Ms. Bean, and *hello*, students."

"Why, hello, Mr. Hornsby. Energetic on this Monday morning, are we?"

"We sure are because today is going to be a very special day."

"Well, okay then." Ms. Bean smiled. "We can all use a bit of that positivity, can't we kids?"

"Hi, Mr. Hornsby," said Michelle.

"Hi, Michelle. How wonderful that I get to cover for one of your classes again. How are you this fine morning?"

"Good."

"Well, I'm thrilled to be with you guys once again on this very special day. Now let's get to it."

Ms. Bean had a confused look and approached. "Get to what?"

"Today, we're going to witness history."

"Actually, we were just about to jump back into our journals to do some writing."

"Perfect. But it will have to wait. With what they're about to witness, they will soon have even more to write about."

"Okay? So what then did you have in mind?"

Hornsby had already taken a seat at the teacher's desk and was logging into his presentation. "Raise a hand if you've ever vacationed at a national park with your families, like this one, Yellowstone." But none of the kids raised hands. "Well, neither have I. But after meeting, I mean, learning more about former president Benjamin Harrison, our twenty-third president, I plan on it, and so should you. Here's a picture of Ben, and now here are some sights in Yellowstone National Park."

"Where's that?" one of the students asked.

"It's in the state of Wyoming. Also, in the state of Wyoming is the Shoshone National Forest. Here are pictures. And here are pictures of the entrance to White River National Forest in Colorado. Aren't you just dying to go visit one of these parks now?" The students nodded. "Well, these lands were first set aside in our country, thanks to a law signed by President Benjamin Harrison in 1891 called the Forest Reserve Act."

"How come?" asked Michelle.

"Because Benjamin had a teacher when he was ten years old who helped him realize the importance of preserving our wonderful land."

"That must have been one wonderful teacher," said Ms. Bean, still appearing puzzled by the direction of the lesson.

"Ms. Bean, isn't it awesome that these lands and the nature that lives on them will forever be saved?"

"Why, yes, Mr. Hornsby. But you never asked me if I visited one of these parks. Kids, my parents took my sister and me to Yellowstone when I was right about your age."

"Do you have pictures?" asked Michelle.

"I do. How about I bring them in? You can see me at your age."

"I'll make sure not to miss it." Hornsby smiled. Then he stood up. With excitement, he asked, "Now who wants to go see President Harrison himself?"

"Ooh, I do."

"I do," another student called out with his hand up.

"But, Mr. Hornsby, you said President Harrison signed this into law in 1891. Isn't he dead by now?" asked Ms. Bean.

"He is. But why not go meet him anyway?"

Ms. Bean was confused. "Okay…"

"Will we be wearing those virtual headset things?" Michelle asked.

"Nope. Even better, you're going to meet the real man himself, but…" Hornsby paused. "Since he's a very important man and he wouldn't want a bunch of kids and teachers just coming up to him, let's keep our distance and be respectful. We are going to watch him sign the Forest Reserve Act into law. But then immediately come right back to our classroom. Okay?"

"Okay," agreed the students.

"Promise?"

"Yes."

Ms. Bean peeked her head out and looked down the hallway, trying to figure out what was going on.

"But you kids first have to do one thing for me, okay?"

"What?"

"We must all hold hands."

"Why?" Michelle asked.

"Because we will always be stronger as a unit than alone. That includes both Ms. Bean and me as well."

"Why are you holding those stickers?" asked one of the students.

Hornsby looked down at the two star stickers. "Oh, these. Someone very important has been waiting a long time for them. Now come on, Ms. Bean, grab hold of my hand and grab Michelle's."

Ms. Bean walked over and whispered, "You okay, Ethan?"

Hornsby offered a bright smile. "Actually, I've never been better."

"Then what's gotten into you?"

Hornsby reached out his hand. "Just grab hold."

"Okay? Now what?"

Hornsby raised his voice, "Come on, kids. Let's make a chain. Ready? Okay. Here we go…"

ABOUT THE AUTHORS

Andrew Brezak is the author of the novels *Lesson Plan* and *The Perfect Answer*. *Mr. Hornsby and the Time-Traveling Classroom* is his first middle-school series. He is a teacher at Sachem North High School on Long Island.

Daniel Brezak is a student at Sachem North High School and a cocreator of the Mr. Hornsby series. His dream is to become a director and looks forward to bringing the Mr. Hornsby series to the television screen.